THE PENGUIN BEST
STORIES OF D'ARCY NILAND

selected with an introduction by RUTH PARK

Penguin Books

Penguin Books Australia Ltd,
487 Maroondah Highway, PO Box 257
Ringwood, Victoria 3134, Australia
Penguin Books Ltd,
Harmondsworth, Middlesex, England
Penguin Books.
40 West 23rd Street, New York, NY 10010, USA
Penguin Books Canada Ltd,
2801 John Street, Markham, Ontario, Canada L3R 1B4
Penguin Books (NZ) Ltd,
182-190 Wairau Road, Auckland 10, New Zealand

This collection first published by Penguin Books Australia, 1987

Typeset in Garamond Book by Leader Composition Pty Ltd
Made and printed in Australia by The Book Printer, Maryborough, Victoria

Niland, D'Arcy, 1920-1967.
The Penguin best stories of D'Arcy Niland.
ISBN 0 14 008927 6.
I. Park, Ruth. II. Title.
A823'.3

Penguin Books

THE PENGUIN BEST STORIES OF D'ARCY NILAND

D'Arcy Niland was born in Glen Innes, New South Wales, and spent much of his boyhood travelling with his Irish father, who followed the New South Wales shearing circuit. He began work as a copyboy on the Sydney *Sun* but decided quite early that in order to write about real people he had to travel, work and live amongst them. Accordingly he led an adventurous, rather romantic life, travelling throughout Australia and the Pacific, working in a wide variety of jobs — as an opal-miner, circus hand, stevedore, woolshed rouseabout and later as a television and film scriptwriter and magazine editor.

He married the writer, Ruth Park and they had five children. D'Arcy Niland died suddenly in 1967 from a heart attack, two days after completing his last novel, *Dead Men Running*. He was forty-seven, and well established as one of Australia's best known novelists. *The Shiralee*, with its insights into fatherhood, confirms that he understood the human heart as well as he knew the country roads of Australia.

CONTENTS

INTRODUCTION
Ruth Park

D'Arcy Niland was the most unusual human being I ever met. Some may think I make this assertion because I was married to the man, but in truth I was, and am, completely detached.

His rare character centred in the fact that never, at any stage of his life did he need to be anything or anyone other than himself. He was as unselfconscious as a bird, and as far as we know birds never ask themselves 'Why aren't I a cow?' or get themselves into a fret analysing their birdness.

When I first met him, when we were nineteen, I realised immediately that here was a Stone Age man. He knew nothing about role-playing, putting on a front, or impressing me or anyone else. He would have died rather than refer to himself as a writer. If pressed, he mumbled 'I write.' Being a writer didn't make him what he was, and he knew it.

He was so honest, so plain, so straightforward that he communicated a kind of innocence. I thing of it as a Celtic innocence, but perhaps that's not accurate.

As a species, we humans tend to hive together, sneaking sidelong glances at anyone different from ourselves. So one might have expected the devious, the insecure, and the mainstream swimmers to avoid him, twitching with discomfort. This was not so. Ten minutes after we had joined any gathering, social or business, I always lost him. He'd be in a corner, with half a dozen people around him. Not talking to him, no. Listening. Somehow people knew that he liked them exactly as they were. They fell over themselves to tell him all about their lives. They never forgot him, either. Years after he died I received airletters and postcards from Memphis, Rome, London and Lightning Ridge that said 'I only spoke with him once or twice, but it's like I always knew him.'

And I remember, too, the morning after his sudden death, when our Italian fruiterer phoned for the weekly order, and I told him what had happened. There was a little silence, and then he said: 'He was my brother.'

D'Arcy Niland was born a writer. Study and untiring practice gave him his craft, and Australia itself his characters, landscape and spirit. The geneses of his stories are to be found on thousands of odds and bobs of paper — railway consignment slips, the backs of telegraph forms, and the miniature notebooks he always carried in his wallet, as others carry business cards. From these literary rags — plot skeletons, waifish words, ideas without tops or tails — he wove his stories. Though for the last decade of his life he had a workroom of his own, mostly he wrote anywhere he found himself. I shake his old manuscripts, and a little dust wisps out — red or golden sand, or the pale mullocky grit from gold or opal field. I sniff a page of beautiful Lilliputian handwriting and catch the ghostly whiff of wintergreen oil. He must have written this story at a shed at Guyra or Narrabri, after rubbing the back of some poor devil of a shearer. He was skilled at rubbing aching backs.

He spent a good deal of his life wandering this continent, but never did it with a return air ticket and a literary grant in his pocket. For him research was doing what his characters did, finding jobs where he could, living on what he earned, travelling with a swag up. His road name was Tom Niland. For Tom Niland the crumbling general store, abandoned when the diggers moved on, 'its walls coloured like the skin of a crocodile' was a place to camp. He camped with the bats and the spiders. And if he wrote about it later it was because that old store was now a part of his own life and history, not because he'd taken a snap of it, written a few descriptive words and put the lot away in a manila folder labelled 'research.'

D'Arcy Niland was a brilliantly educated man who had had only primary school education. Somehow the nuns of St Joseph's, Glen Innes, hammered or prayed into him the way to achieve learning. He was astonishingly well-read, and not only in English. In middle age he learned Italian so he could read Elsa Morante in the original. Also he was not altogether satisfied with D.H. Lawrence's free translation of Giavanni Verga. However, English was his love. He had a vocabulary so large I was never able to trip him, even with the aid of Ogilvie's Obsolete. Some of this ardour for the English language must have been genetic and familial. Certainly he had a poor and difficult background, though it troubled him not at all. About it he once said 'Other people had warm clothing and the best cuts of meat, but we had the words.' This was true. His family's day-to-day conversation was straight out of Behan and Myles na Coppaleen. In more tumultuous moments it became pure Synge.

There is a myth that D'Arcy Niland was born in Ireland. Even the Irish believe it. Once in a Dublin bookshop I found his novel *The Shiralee*. The bookshop commented: 'He's one of us, of course, but didn't someone take the poor fella off to the colonies when he was a chiselur.'

Still, he was indeed Irish, very Celtic to look at, and with pure Irish ancestry. The Nilands were originally a cadet branch of the great O'Neills, Owen Roe and all that wild lot. After Cromwell, many of them drifted down into Galway, where some still live. The Famine drove the rest across Ireland to Dublin.

The first Tom Niland arrived as a bounty immigrant to Sydney in 1841. He lived in Pitt Street, and instantly found a job as a cooper. Very soon he and his wife Mary settled on the Northern Rivers, where they established a long and respected line of coopers and timber millers. All of these men and women married other Irish people. Their descendant, D'Arcy's father Francis Niland, married a girl much closer to the old sod. Her mother was born in Callan, and her father in King's County, now called Offaly.

D'Arcy Niland himself was born in Glen Innes in 1917. The Callan grandmother delivered him. She was a bush nurse with the strong, saintly face often seen on religious Irishwomen whose husbands are fiends out of hell. Which the King's County William certainly was. This old woman lived with the Niland family. She was very close to her young grandson.

In a way my first six years were spent in the shadow of Slievenamon. I knew it meant the Hill of the Woman, and I thought Granny was that woman. She had more stories than Hans Andersen, and she told me all of them.

Granny Egan predicted he would grow up to be a bishop but he stood out firmly against that idea. By the time he was eight, he was making up stories. By twelve years old, he wanted to be published. He informed his friend Sister Mary Roch that he was going to be a writer. Many years later she confessed that she could have cried. She knew that this clever boy with the home-cut hair and the unlucky family did not have a chance in the world of ending as anything but a farm labourer or a rouseabout in a shearing shed.

The country was already perishing in the Depression — families evicted and living in bag huts on waste land; whole flocks driven to the boiling-down works; every third shop

4

abandoned and boarded-up; white-collar workers with soft hands ravenous foɪ casual work — rabbiting, dingo-baiting, thistle-cutting. New South Wales belonged 'to the Banks and the crows'.

Sydney, where the family presently migrated in search of work, was not much better, except that it belonged 'to the Banks and the rats'. The city was so run-down the creatures could be seen in daylight, foraging fiercely in the gutters. But there was night school, the Public Library and Paddy's Market, where a boy on fire for knowledge could find thousands of battered old books for tuppence and even a penny.

I think I was half crazy. I stayed up all night reading and writing, walking around that rat-ridden backyard, full of old prams and rotting wood and a century's junk, looking at the stars, praying, saying poetry to myself, crying sometimes because I knew there was something I had to do, had to find out, and I didn't know what it was and there was no one to ask.

Only the books. Sometimes I didn't have the tuppence, and the stallholder would hunt me out of there for standing around reading the stock. But Paddy's was the beginning for me. There I found translations of the great European short story writers, and lightning struck me.

He had already spent years studying the Australian writers as Sister Roch and others had advised him. He had taken Henry Lawson and the others to pieces and tried to put them together again.

But it wasn't until I read the French, Hungarian, Russian writers that I realised the Australians, and the English, too, weren't writing real short stories at all. What they were producing were vignettes, and landscape or character studies. Or sketches. Early Katherine Mansfield stuff. What the Americans call *pieces*.

This misconception, far from peculiar to Australian writing, still prevails. But a short story is not a story that is short; it is a literary form as precise and as elegant as a sonnet.

The boy reacted almost violently. 'Tolstoy, de Maupassant, Isak Babel! I was in a state of shock for days. Because I'd suspected it somehow, the shape of these European stories. A strong shape, like a tree. Not at all like Henry Lawson or the others.'

He turned his face and mind to what he could now learn. He is, therefore, one of the very few Australian writers who wrote classic short stories, European in form and technique, though they are about Australian subjects and people.

I stayed up all night and wrote a little story in this style new to me. I wasn't quite sixteen, and had no ideas of markets. Would you believe it, I sent it to 'Sunbeams', the children's page in the *Sun*.

Twenty years afterwards, I met Marie Marshall, long retired. As Cousin Marie, she had edited 'Sunbeams'. These are her words:

The story was called *Help* and was obviously the work of an experienced writer. I thought at once that this rotten kid had plagiarised someone else's published story, and I made up my mind to have his hide for it.

She wrote to D'Arcy Niland asking him to come and see her.

Plagiarism or copying wasn't all that uncommon amongst the children. Usually I would recognise the poem or story at once, though I didn't recognise *Help*. I was going to give this Niland boy a good scare. Anyway, in he came, good-looking, awkward, soaked to the skin. It was raining, and although I didn't know it of course, he had no coat to his name. He showed me three or four other stories he'd written since *Help*. I looked through them, and there was no doubt — this dripping youngster had written *Help*. Of course the story was no use to the children's page, so I showed it and the others to some of my newspaper colleagues. The upshot was that he was recommended for a cadetship. They started him off as a copyboy.

The cadetship never materialised. On the horizon was the dark shadow of war, which tends to eat young men, so all the newspapers became wary of taking on youthful staff. D'Arcy Niland kept on writing, sometimes being published. He made a meagre living doing casual proofreading. The war started, he attended for his Army physical, and the doctor told him his heart wasn't altogether normal, but that it would never bother him. He forgot about it, married the present writer, and together we scraped out a living freelancing. Hard, hard times, but mostly I remember laughing my head off, for D'Arcy was a very funny young man. For some of the stories in this Penguin collection he was paid ten shillings, which did not pay for a room and shared cooking arrangements even then.

Life moved on, he kept on writing, and achieved a modest success. Of course he did have to write the hated 'pieces'; radio plays, journalistic assignments, even novels which scared him as nothing else did. They were too broad, not condensed enough, a man lost the form while he was covering that enormous canvas — he wasn't a novelist but a short story writer. Even when *The Shiralee* was a smash hit, winning many international awards, putting a new word into the language, he scarcely paid attention, being away on the opal field at Andamooka, hoping to get enough material for some short stories.

At almost forty years of age, his heart knocked hard on his chest, and he almost died. When he was better we decided he should go on living the way he was born to, as a writer. So he did, never losing his good humour, full of jokes and liveliness. We went back to Ireland and lived there for a little in the neighbourhood of misty, mysterious Slievenamon. We went too, to that 'quiet watered land, a land of roses', a little place of grey monastic ruins, Clonmacnois. It is in the very centre of Ireland. Nothing there at all, really, but leaning tombstones, blowing grass, and swans sailing on a small young Shannon. The air full of that fugitive, unearthly light that to me means Ireland.

D'Arcy said: 'I think I'll come and blow about here after I'm dead.'

I went back a few years ago but he wasn't there, only the swans and the light.

He died in 1967, a few days after he finished the novel *Dead Men Running*. He belonged to Australia as well as to Ireland, and in the end Australia took him. He did what the woman in his story *Away to Moonlight* decided to do:

I'm going to work till I drop. Going to die with my blood hot.

Fall down on the earth and die.

THE PARACHUTIST

*T*he hurricane came down from Capricorn, and for two days and a night it rained.

In the darkness of the second night, softening away to dawn, there was silence. There was only the gurgle and drip of the wet world, and the creatures that lived on the earth began to appear, freed from the tyranny of the elements.

The hawk, ruffled in misery, brooding in ferocity, came forth in hunger and hate.

It struck off into the abyss of space, scouring the earth for some booty of the storm — the sheep lying like a heap of wet kapok in the sodden paddocks, the bullock like a dark bladder carried down on the swollen stream and washing against a tree on the river flats, the rabbit, driven from its flooded warren and squeezed dead against a log.

With practised eye it scrutinised the floating islands of rubble and the wracks of twigs lying aslew on the banks for sign of lizard or snake, dead or alive. But there was nothing. Once, in the time before, there had been a rooster, a daggled, forlorn derelict riding a raft of flotsam: too weak to fight and too sick to care about dying or the way it died.

The hawk rested on a crag of the gorge and conned the

terrain with a fierce and frowning eye. The lice worried its
body with the sting of nettles. Savagely it plucked with its
beak under the fold of its wings, first on one side, then on the
other. It rasped its bill on the jagged stone, and dropped over
the lip. It climbed in a gliding circle, widening its field of
vision.

The earth was yellow and green. On the flats were chains of
lagoons as if the sky had broken and fallen in sheets of blue
glass. The sun was hot and the air heavy and humid.

Swinging south, the hawk dropped over a vast graveyard of
dead timber. The hurricane had ravaged the gaunt trees,
splitting them, falling them, tearing off their naked arms and
strewing the ground with pieces, like a battlefield of bones,
grey with exposure and decay.

A rabbit sprang twenty yards like a bobbing wheel, and the
sight drew the hawk like a plummet, but the rabbit vanished in
a hollow log, and stayed there, and there was no other life.

Desperate, weak, the hawk alighted on a bleak limb and
glared in hate. The sun was a fire on its famished body. Logs
smoked with steam and the brightness of water on the earth
reflected like mirrors. The telescopic eye inched over the
ground — crawled infallibly over the ground, and stopped.
And then suddenly the hawk swooped to the ground and tore
at the body of a dead field mouse — its belly bloated and a
thin vapor drifting from the grey, plastered pelt.

The hawk did not sup as it supped on the hot running blood
of the rabbit in the trap — squealing in eyeless terror; it did
not feast in stealthy leisure as it did on the sheep paralysed in
the drought, tearing out bit by bit its steaming entrails.
Voraciously it ripped at the mouse, swallowing fast and
finishing the meal in a few seconds.

But the food was only a tantalisation, serving to make the
hawk's appetite more fierce, more lusty. It flew into a tree,
rapaciously scanning the countryside. It swerved into space
and climbed higher and higher in a vigilant circle, searching
the vast expanse below, even to its uttermost limits.

Hard to the west something moved on the earth, a speck: and the hawk watched it: and the speck came up to a walnut, and up to a plum, and up to a ball striped with white and grey.

The hawk did not strike at once. Obedient to instinct, it continued to circle, peering down at the farmhouse and the outbuildings, suspicious; seeing the draught horses in the yard and fowls in the hen coop, the pigs in the sty, and the windmill twirling, and watching for human life in their precincts.

Away from them all, a hundred yards or more, down on the margin of the fallowed field, the kitten played, leaping and running and tumbling, pawing at a feather and rolling on its back biting at the feather between its forepaws.

Frenzied with hunger, yet ever cautious, the hawk came down in a spiral, set itself, and swooped. The kitten propped and froze with its head cocked on one side, unaware of danger but startled by this new and untried sport. It was no more than if a piece of paper had blown past it in a giant brustle of sound. But in the next moment the hawk fastened its talons in the fur and the fat belly of the kitten, and the kitten spat and twisted, struggling against the power that was lifting it.

Its great wings beating, paddling with the rhythm of oars, the hawk went up a slope of space with its cargo, and the kitten, airborne for the first time in its life, the earth running under it in a blur, wailed in shrill terror. It squirmed frantically as the world fell away in the distance, but the hawk's talons were like steel grabs.

The air poured like water into the kitten's eyes and broke against its face, streaming back against its rippling furry sides. It howled in infinite fear, and gave a sudden desperate twist, so that the hawk was jolted in its course and dropped to another level, a few feet below the first.

Riding higher and higher on the wind, the hawk went west by the dam like a button of silver far below. The kitten cried now with a new note. Its stomach was wambling. The air gushing into its mouth and nostrils set up a humming in its ears and an aching dizziness in its head. As the hawk turned on its soundless orbit, the sun blazed like flame in the kitten's eyes, leaving its sight to emerge from a blinding greyness.

The kitten knew that it had no place here in the heart of space, and its terrified instincts told it that its only contact with solidity and safety was the thing that held it.

Then the hawk was ready to drop its prey. It was well practised. Down had gone the rabbit, a whistle in space, to crash in a quiver of death on the ruthless earth. And the hawk had followed to its gluttonous repast.

Now there at two thousand feet the bird hovered. The kitten was alarmingly aware of the change, blinking at the pulsations of beaten air as the wings flapped, hearing only that sound. Unexpectedly, it stopped, and the wings were still — outstretched, but rigid, tilting slightly with the poised body, only the fanned tail lifting and lowering with the flow of the currents.

The kitten felt the talons relax slightly, and that was its warning. The talons opened, but in the first flashing shock of the movement the kitten completed its twist and slashed at the hawk's legs and buried its claws in the flesh like fish-hooks. In the next fraction of a second the kitten had consolidated its position, securing its hold, jabbing in every claw except those on one foot which thrust out in space, pushing against insupportable air. And then the claws on this foot were dug in the breast of the hawk.

With a cry of pain and alarm the bird swooped crazily, losing a hundred feet like a dropping stone. And then it righted itself, flying in a drunken sway that diminished as it circled.

Blood from its breast beaded and trickled down the paw of the kitten and spilled into one eye. The kitten blinked, but the blood came and congealed, warm and sticky. The kitten could not turn its head. It was frightened to risk a change of position. The blood slowly built over its eye a blinding pellicle.

The hawk felt a spasm of weakness, and out of it came an accentuation of its hunger and a lust to kill at all costs the victim it had claimed and carried to this place of execution. Lent an access of power by its ferocity, it started to climb again, desperately trying to dislodge the kitten. But the weight was too much and it could not ascend. A great tiredness came in its dragging body; an ache all along the frames of its wings. The kitten clung tenaciously, staring down at the winding earth and mewling in terror.

For ten minutes the hawk gyrated on a level, defeated and bewildered. All it wanted to do now was to get rid of the burden fastened to its legs and body. It craved respite, a spell on the tallest trees, but it only flew high over these trees, knowing it was unable to perch. Its beak gaped under the harsh ruptures of its breath. It descended three hundred feet. The kitten, with the wisdom of instinct, never altered its position, but rode down like some fantastic parachutist.

In one mighty burst the hawk with striking beak and a terrible flapping of its wings tried finally to cast off its passenger — and nearly succeeded. The kitten miauled in a frenzy of fear at the violence of the sound and the agitation. Its back legs dangled in space, treading air, and like that it went around on the curves of the flight for two minutes. Then it secured a foothold again, even firmer than the first.

In a hysterical rage, the hawk tried once more to lift itself, and almost instantly began to sweep down in great, slow, gliding eddies that became narrower and narrower.

The kitten was the pilot now and the hawk no longer the assassin of the void, the lord of the sky and the master of the wind. The ache coiled and throbbed in its breast. It fought against the erratic disposition of its wings and the terror of its waning strength. Its heart bursting with the strain, its eyes dilated wild and yellow, it came down until the earth skimmed under it; and the kitten cried at the silver glare of the roofs not far off, and the expanding earth, and the brush of the grass.

13

The hawk lobbed and flung over, and the kitten rolled with it. And the hawk lay spraddled in exhaustion, its eyes fiercely, cravenly aware of the danger of its forced and alien position.

The kitten staggered giddily, unhurt, towards the silver roofs, wailing loudly as if in answer to the voice of a child.

THE BOY IN THE DARK

*T*en thousand machines had stopped, a thousand
fires were banked, a million cogs had come to rest, tongue in
groove and sprocket in link: miles of belts had ceased their
slapping rolling, and the fly-wheels were dead: the smoke was
dying from the mouths of chimneys, and all this was that much
noise and energy suspended. And yet the streets were thick
with the maze of workers, the night shifts going and the day
shifts returning. The trams were grinding and clanging, full,
and the drays and waggons and cars were packing the shop-
embanked roads. There was greater noise and greater energy.
This was the burst and the second wind, the top gear of the Big
Smoke.

The kid dawdled around the corner, the loaf of bread under
his arm. He passed the wine bar and heard the dynamo in
there. Sometimes he thought of the doors flying open and a
cloud of insects hurtling out thick as rain and still humming
and skirling. At other times he imagined a bit of the surf
trapped and washing in there; the same that you see on the
beach at Clovelly and Coogee.

A dog welcomed a lamp-post, and the kid thought he would
do that sometime, too, and see what it was like. One thing

about dogs, they didn't have to wear pants. If dogs had pants he thought, how would they undo their buttons?

The girls from the chocolate factory, in green smocks and red caps, clattered past him, laughing and chattering. He started to cross the road, going around the head of a horse. He looked at the big, long head, and into the warm dark eyes like brown glass, and at the salivary rubber of the lips, and he saw the square flecks of chaff caught there, and he remembered that that was something else he had to try sometime: see what chaff tasted like.

The cracked road had oozed with a black gelatinous blood of pitch from the flame of the day, and he squiggled his big toe in the molten bleeding. Up on a balcony an elderly man leaned on his elbows, looking to be just top and arms, and peered down at the cavalcade. There were dogs like him that sat that way at kennel mouths.

The kid kicked at a heap of manure and sent it scattering in all directions, and climbed on to the kerb. The elderly man coughed and the kid looked up: 'Good-day, Mister Draper.'

The man didn't answer. The answer was in his eyes. The kid felt the slight, and he hated Draper, and wished he hadn't spoken. He wanted to get the words back and stick them wherever words belonged inside him and spit out others to tease or anger the man, or to say nothing.

He sauntered up past the school, and away over him and around him and beyond him as far as he could hear there was the familiarity of din and racket. A youthful printer, grimed with his trade, bolted past him to catch a tram, and his bolting was a smear of noise and a wind. A bottle-capper whistled loudly and it was like the warble of a bird. The traffic in slow converging rivers of movement stopped, shook impatience from themselves, and started. Suddenly a billycart screeched at his nerves, and he jerked around to see it, driven by a nine-year-old freak in goggles, tear past him and scorch the asphalt with the doubled and redoubled echo of falling skittles.

A loosely-wired drunk staggered along the kerb, telling the world why he didn't want to live: The world's in a mess, and it won't be long before the bloody Kaiser's right here in this town, and all the statues of Queen Victoria for miles around wearing spiked helmets.

The boy wondered at him curiously.

He got off the main thoroughfare and entered a lane. There was no diminution of the sound. There was only the sensation of having come from the midst of it on to the sidelines of it. This crash and boom and pace of a million units and a billion decibels was the slate of his brain and his life was written on it.

He came to the church and there he stopped, only momentarily, for he turned and went up the worn steps, hollowed like spoons. He merely diverted himself from the course of his path home with the easefulness of a river following the channel it had been scoring for centuries. He hadn't made any decision. The decision had been made weeks, months, before.

It wasn't strange. Unkajoe had always brought him as far as the church steps, and, with stern admonitions not to leave before Mass was over, had left him. And he had gone in. He always sat at the back of the church and looked at the people coming in and watched them slipping their coins into the poorbox. And when he slowly drifted out at the end of Mass, he watched then, too, the coins being put in, and he got to know the sound.

There was the empty sound of the echo of threepence on wood; there was the clunk of the half-full mark; there was the brief, almost instantaneous peck of evidence when the box was full.

He knew all that. He'd thought about the box. He'd had it in his hands, spilling its treasures and loading his pockets till they bulged and pulled the waistline from under his belt with the weight. He had walked into shops and pointed to sweets and toys and cricket bats and footballs with the air of a millionaire ordering diamonds. He desperately wanted the

17

things he coveted. He had bestowed fruits and drinks on the kids he knew and had found favour with them to the peak of his desire.

All that had been done except that it hadn't been achieved. All it wanted was the impulse, and this was the moment of impulse.

As he went through the Gothic door into the cool barrel of the church, he knew that it was the right time, the fall of evening, and he knew that he would be successful. He could feel it in the beat of his blood, the excited lilt of his heart, and the delight of the adventure in his quick mentations.

The church was empty. Nothing, to his mind, was ever so empty as an empty church. It wasn't empty because there were no people in it. That didn't make it empty. It had the look and the air of just emptiness. It was a building housing emptiness, as if emptiness were something concrete though intangible.

He knelt in the back pew and looked ahead over the uniform rows of thick, warm-brown, wooden seats, polished to show his fingers in their reflecting surface. There was red light burning on a mount in the sanctuary. It wasn't a red lamp, he knew. It was a red, open glass globe with a candle sitting deep in its middle. But it looked like a red lamp. The flame bobbed in a tapering bud and fluttered like a golden moth caught there.

When his eye came to Christ being taken down from the cross, the thirteenth station, he looked at the red blood from the side wound, and he remembered the time he nicked his finger with a pocket knife to see if he bled red, too. He had expected to bleed black, and he was surprised and happy and yet mystified at the difference between himself and white children and yet the sameness there in the blood.

The highly-polished brass rails surmounting the marble fence that divided the sanctuary from the body of the church glowed dark yellow, and the point of a knob where a wayward ray ricocheted and struck it became a burst of dazzling cusps.

High along the walls of the church the oblong windows of stained glass glowed with red and green, purple, jargoon and mazarine in the coloured raiment of the saints depicted there. Through one window, towards the western altar of the Virgin Mary, the sun rays were diagonal blazes, vanes of differing intensities: nearer him they were golden poles leaning against the windows at the source of their being and at the end of space they broke on a pew and on the floor in a sprawl of golden ink.

The boy blessed himself, genuflected, and hurried over to the wall at the back of the church. He looked at the poorbox. It was frail. He looked all round him. Then he took out his penknife. He heard someone approaching, the weary scuff of broken shoes on the stone steps, and he walked quickly back to the pew.

A woman came in and walked tiredly and piously down the aisle, and knelt there in the middle with her head on one side.

'Damn woman,' the boy said. 'Hurry up, hurry up, hurry up, silly old woman.'

He was still excited and the obstruction of this woman only added to the thrilled sensation. In a few minutes she went out and the boy hastened to the box. He stood there for a moment looking around him at the dimming rays and the brightening scarlet of the sanctuary lamp.

Then he heard a door slam. A priest in his cassock came out of the vestry, walked to the centre of the altar and genuflected, then turned; and the boy, for the first time feeling the nag of frustration, acted. He thought quickly, or rather he did not think at all. He followed the line of his ambition. He didn't scurry back to the pew or skip out the door. He darted quickly to the left, into the porch, and found himself on the dark steps of the stairs that twisted to the loft.

He stood there, and as the priest came down the aisle the boy noiselessly went higher, up around the bend of the stairs, and waited, big-eyed with guilty pleasure and expectancy.

He could hear the priest in the porch, and he heard the

heavy stridulation of the closing door. He heard it jolt into place. He heard the rasp of the bolts and the grating turn of the key. He waited. He bumped down the stairs on his seat, slowly and cautiously, and watched the priest enter the sanctuary, genuflect, and disappear into the vestry. He heard the slam of the vestry door. He sat on the bottom step.

He was smiling.

In a few minutes he had opened the box with his penknife. He scraped with both hands, fisting out the money and cramming it into his pockets. Then he went to the door and dragged at the bolts. He got one free, and then the other, but the door, he confirmed, was locked. He went down into the vestry and tried the door there. It, too, was locked.

He was still smiling, though a little unsurely.

He realised that this was his chance to see what the church looked like from the pulpit. He stood looking over the circular rail, and the darkening emptiness looked back. He walked up the aisle, peering at the windows with their sloping sills. They were too high to reach.

In the last pew at the back he sat down. He was working it out, and he decided to sit through the night there. It was easy. He was smart. He'd go to sleep in the organ loft and when the priest came in the morning to open the door he'd come down secretly and go off. And if someone saw him they would only think he was present at morning Mass.

That would do fine.

But wait a minute. What about the bread for tea, and Unkajoe? They'll start looking and they won't find me.

He screwed up his face and bit his finger and thought. He liked the spice of danger in his enterprise, the risk, even the sense of guilt. He knew which was the bigger end of the dilemma. And he decided that he wouldn't be worried about spending the night in the church.

He began to eat the soft inside out of the loaf.

To find out where he might sleep, he went up into the organ loft, leaned over the rail and looked down into the body of the church. He was surprised to see there the woolly grey darkness that welled up like a fog. It was as though the darkness started at the floor and worked up. The upper air was a lighter void. But the gloom was saturating that, too. The way he saw it, the light was leaving the church, flowing back the way it came, going out through the glass of the windows because that's where the last of it lingered and died.

Soon the creeping darkness had filled the whole church. There was a ghostly fugitive shine on the organ pipes, like an optical illusion. The boy peered all around him. Then he went down to try the door again. He went to the vestry door. He saw the surplices of the altar boys bulkily hanging on the walls like limp and headless beings. He didn't like the start it gave him, but he felt the cloth and said: 'Silly old things.'

Slowly, he walked into the transept, staring. Here, prisoner with him, was black space, and the black space filled with faint sounds, magnified by his blindness. It seemed to him a solid block of darkness with the red light beaming in the sanctuary. He hoped it wouldn't go out. The darkness had no locality; he felt he was lost, and he wondered how big he was. He felt very little and helpless in the distortion of its immensity. He was walking about in a cave, the pitch-dark caves that Unkajoe talked about; then he was in a grave, a vast grave.

He sat down in one of the pews and looked with a beginning fear at the dark. It was so close to him it was in his mouth. Outside the city washed against the church in sound, but with the remoteness of bells in a dream and with the loneliness of the sea on midnight costs.

It began to get cold. He curled his legs under his backside. He thought if he closed his eyes it wouldn't be so bad, because he would be as dark as the darkness. It was being open-eyed with only darkness to see that was bad.

He shut his eyes.

He saw the black panther with the green eyes at the bottom of the tree, and the man skulking in the branches, his face glistening with sweat; the beast swishing its tail and leaping with claws unsheathed and ripping streaks out of the tree trunk as it fell back to earth. And the man was Unkajoe. And he saw a figure that was himself running through the forest and coming upon the panther, wrestling with it over and over in a roll, thrusting its jaws away and then burying the knife in its throat, and the blood coming red on its pulsing breast.

The wind thrummed under the door. He jerked his eyes open, fright in his stomach. He peered all about him, and dense blackness held the secret of what it hid.

He got up and walked down towards the red light. He was afraid now; sober-faced. He felt the cold grip his ankles; the draught swim around his legs as though he was paddling in it.

There was a birling whistle high up in the wall, and it stopped him in his tracks. He peered into the darkness, losing his breath.

His eyes were big.

The whistle came intermittently, and searching for the reason, he put it down to a crack in the window that caught the rising wind.

But he wanted to get out.

He went to the back of the church and again tried the door. He stared in fright. There was something behind him. It was hiding in the darkness. He craned his neck. There was nothing.

He placed his hand out and it touched the cold, lifeless foot of a statue. He moved off a few yards and looked back. The statue was following. He waited, then sneaked his hand out again, but it wasn't there. He swallowed the dry spit in his throat.

Down in the middle of the church there was a congress of currents, a slight wail set up by the clumsy romp of the draughts.

Terror started where fear left off.

God sees you. He heard the sister saying it. This is God's house, and he sees you no matter what you do. He sees you always.

The saints were talking. They were whispering. They had swords and spears and they were talking about how to deal with him. They would tie him to a post and light a fire under him. They would turn him into a pillar of salt. They were thinking it out. They were down in the middle there.

As he looked a saint came through the darkness with a dead-white face, the eyes glaring, and stood off a few yards, hating him, and then vanished. The boy felt himself being watched and he flung his head around and saw out of the tail of his eye a face blur in the darkness and disappear.

Then he thought of the devil. The devil was in this church.

And the boy hoarsely whispered, looking at the altar: 'The devil told me to do it.'

He went back to the poorbox and quickly pulled the coins out of his pockets and emptied them with a clang and clatter into the box. And he waited to see if he felt better: and he couldn't hear the conspiracy of saints, he wasn't being watched, the devil was gone.

Then he heard the creak of a pew, the cry of timber, and he stood stockstill. He was looking down towards the sanctuary, listening. He heard footsteps. They were coming up the aisle on the left. Slowly and carefully. The boy found the aisle on the right, half ran along it and propped like a kangaroo and listened. The pew was creaking as though something, someone, was crossing from left to right. Then the footsteps came down the aisle he was in.

He was now driven to silence in the guardianship of his instincts, and he sneaked quickly around by the altar rails and went up the left aisle. When he heard the footsteps opposite him in the other aisle he pelted quickly as he could towards the back of the church, and panting, looked down towards the sanctuary lamp. He saw the light black out and reappear as though something solid passed it.

He was crying without a sound, a whimpering grunting that he hushed as quickly as it rose.

Then he heard the sound coming up the aisle towards him,

23

the slap of feet treading softly. He was near a statue and he stood hard against it, completely still. The feet came up, stopped. The boy heard the breathing a man makes sleeping with his mouth open. It was only a yard or so away from him. He bit on his hand. The scream choked, suffocated by fear, in his throat. The footsteps passed on around the aisle again.

Now the boy began to shake with terror. He felt towards a pew and knelt, and started to whisper hoarsely: 'I won't do it again. True, I won't do it again. The devil put me up to it, like sister says.'

He went on praying. Then he broke off as he felt the vibration against his knees. Something was moving from the other end along the kneeler. The boy bolted into the aisle and almost ran. He stopped panting, a horrible mateship of tears and shocked breathing coming from him. Why couldn't this thing find him, if it was pure and holy? Why couldn't it go straight to him? It was blundering and groping like some terrible animal, relying on its sense of smell. It was a shaggy blind monster.

The boy waited for his ears to report to him again. But it was ten minutes before he heard anything. He knew the wind now, bumbling under the door, whistling high in the wall. He couldn't stir. He couldn't run wild. He knew he might collide with it. He had to wait until he knew where it was before he could retreat.

He knew where he had last left the thing was at the back of the church, and his eyes and all his hearing were trained in that direction. But the sound came from behind him. The slip-slap of feet, much fainter, more of a measured slither. He had not heard them pass him. It was as if they had left the floor and floated and been set down beyond him.

With a sob he stumbled the length of the aisle, and into the porch, and up the staircase leading to the loft.

He waited there with straining ears filled with the sounds of a sea-shell. Half an hour went by. He moved and stumbled and rushed into himself again. The darkness clothed the monster.

24

He saw it three times, behind and above and before him, but it was a chimera.

Then he heard the slow-gaited footsteps ascending the stairs. He crouched down. He heard the new sound on the bare boards of the loft.

Everything in him roared into his mouth and came out in pealing screams.

Even so, with the dreadful noise in his own ears, he heard the sudden agitation of feet. A grip came on his shirt. And, still shrieking, he kicked out, clutched, and jerked away, and cried out for his mother, though he had had no mother for five years now, and hauled himself on to the balcony rail and fell with the scream changing and stopping dead.

The church was flooded with the radiance of one light after another snapping on, and the priest that came running into the sanctuary from the vestry with a white-faced stare ready to be pinned on the cause of that stare saw nothing, saw emptiness; but he hurried up the aisle, and his eyes fixed themselves with a start on the crumpled body of the boy behind the last pew with a mutilated loaf of bread beside him.

AWAY TO MOONLIGHT

*T*his is a name without a place. That's what they say, and they've been saying it for a long time. But it's a place to me, a belonging, and that's why I came, and that's why I'm here.

My father reared me. He scrubbed me in bush creeks and fed me from a tin plate. He said: 'You'll come with me everywhere, all over the Boomerang. Where I am you will be, always.' I sat around camp fires with him. I curled against his warm body under the sky. I never wore no dresses. I wore boy's clothes, and I looked like a boy. He told me stories, and I asked him questions. He said the world went around like a wheel, but he never knew why. He said the sun was so profitable that men would sell it if only they could work out a way. He took me with him to shearing sheds, vineyards, timber camps, talc mines, canefields, banana plantations, and I grew up that way and became his mate and the woman who did for him.

He was like a whip, tough. I didn't realize how little he was till they brought him up out of the shaft, dead. He fell down there in the darkness, coming home from the rum party at the storekeeper's. He had nothing; only a little parcel of opal. I was twenty then. I lived on there, gouging and working his shaft and mine. I worked it out.

When a stranger came there, I showed him the ropes. He had no money, no gear, nowhere to sleep. I gave him a little hessian shelter at the back of the hut. He ate with me sometimes. We played cards at night. We played for matches. Then kisses. I didn't want no kisses, and I told him. He laughed.

He said: 'I bet it would be like tangling with barbed wire to tangle with you.'

He was a short, well-built man, with quick eyes and a beard that grew black in a day. He called to me one night and I went in. He was sitting on the bunk, taking off his boots. He looked up and said: 'Will you marry me?'

He stood up and put his arms around me. 'I want you,' he said in my ear, close. 'You don't know how much.'

'I've got to think about it.'

'Think about it now. You can't go on like this all your life. There's got to be a man in it for you sometime.'

That was right. There would be a man for me. I would know him when I saw him. Or would I know him? I didn't know whether I was pretending to myself. All my life I might wait. I could wait, too, if I knew. I didn't know, and when I thought I was like a fairy princess waiting for a prince I felt foolish and lonely, because I was no princess and princes don't come to women like me.

I would make a life with this man.

He said that next time he went into town he would make arrangements. In the meantime he said he didn't see any harm in moving in with me and having me be a wife to him. But I told him no. I let him kiss me, I let him touch me, but I fought him back. I struggled to keep the fence between us, but it was hard for me, too. He got sulky and fierce, and then he laughed and told me what a hell of a torment a woman could be.

I felt uneasy, confused. When I went along to the store the boss asked me when the wedding was coming off. The woman said I had a good man, we'd make a good match. I felt proud and happy. I felt I wasn't alone. I knew I belonged.

Then it was straightened out, but not by my doing. A woman came to the field, putting in her two weeks' holiday there with her father. She was good-looking in the way of the city women. I know men, or some men. It is mating season all the time for them. He went off with this woman when she left.

I thought about that good-looking woman. I didn't have white slim hands like hers. I never had a body so slender. My hair, it was black, the same, but I was never able to put it up the way she put hers. She had a soft voice. I tried to say words like she said them. I couldn't.

The months went by and he came back, stringy and burned black and he came up to my door and pushed it open like it was home always.

'I missed you,' he said.

'Storekeeper might fix you up for a place and some food.' You say that to a stranger and he was a stranger.

'I made a mistake.' He meant it. 'She was never the one to last. Not like you. Solid. A man's mate. Be with me again, will you?'

I thought of the good things in him and I still loved them, like you get to love a kitten for its ways. He wanted to live with me. He wanted me to be a woman and a wife to him, only without a ring on my finger. I didn't want no more truck with him that laid on her lean hips. He would float like thistledown again if there was another woman.

'Down there on the rise — that's the storekeeper.' I pointed from the door. 'He'll fix you up.'

He shrugged and went out.

A man came to the field. He was tall and strong with a good face. He had a voice that carried a mile. When I saw him, I said: 'This man is mine. I will take him away from every woman here.'

I met him in the store, and I asked him to my place for tea. I went out in the afternoon and shot a rabbit, and when he came I gave him the choicest parts baked the colour of syrup. We played cards after tea. We played for matches. Then I told him we would play for kisses. I meant it for a joke, but he looked startled, then he laughed and said that would do for him. I told him to get out; what did he think I was?

He put up his hands: 'Hey, wait a minute. You suggested it. What's the game? I wouldn't have dreamt of saying a thing like that.'

'You was ready enough to snap me up.'

'Well, of course — any man would be.'

'And you thought me cheap.'

'Hold on. Not me. If I wanta kiss you I'll kiss you, and it won't be on the turn of a card. You invited me to your place and I come respectable with respectable intentions. Now you just stop this playing up and sit down and deal. And let it be for matches.'

I was certain then. He came every night, to play cards and talk. He came from Snowy River way, and he had had a cut at everything from breaking horses to working in the city. He had done with the city for good. He liked the backwoods. He struck a good patch of opal and made money.

When he came up that night and I got the cards I told him we would play for kisses.

'No bloody fear,' he said.

'I mean it.'

He looked at me. Then he grabbed my hand and pulled me on to his knee. He said: 'You're a wild thing. I could run you down and put my brand on you.'

'We'd better play for matches,' I said.

He hurt his leg and thought he had broken a bone in his foot. He went into town and was gone three weeks. He sent me a letter. 'I can't wait to see you again,' he wrote. 'I want to look at you with your hair hanging to your shoulders and blowing around your face the way it does. I want to see your eyes . . .'

And when I read there was a great surge of love in my heart for this man, a love like the surge of waters. But I looked at my calloused hands like a man's. At the fine wrinkles like a weave of a basket about my eyes. The soles of my feet were leather pads. I smelled of sweat and the earth. I was hard-fleshed, and my breasts were small and like muscles. I was not worthy of this man.

I heard a man singing in the night. I knew it wasn't Jim. He kicked the door open and stayed there. His shirt was open down to his belly. The hair was wet on his chest. He came in holding the bottle. I wasn't frightened of him. I seen men drunk and sober, doing what men do the way men do it, being men. He was that way.

'Think he's better than me, don'tcha? Throw me out and take him on. I'll show you who owns you.'

I didn't want to hurt him. I knew him in drink. I understood him, but I didn't feel nothing for him, not even pity. He lurched across the floor and tried to grab me as I stood up and faced him.

'I want you,' he said, eyes wild and lips wet. 'Christ know how I want you. And I'm gonna have you. You can't kick me out like a dog. I was good to you.'

'Go back to your hut, Mac,' I told him.

His face crumpled. 'You think you can drop me for him — just like that. You're nothing but a slut.'

I went to the door and pushed it open. 'Go. Now.'

He rushed and grabbed me. 'I'll take you,' he yelled. 'I'll have you if it's the last thing I do. You can't treat me like dirt.'

I jerked my head down, smashing it on the bridge of his nose. I know where it hurts a man to be kneed, and I brought up my knee. He rolled on the floor groaning. I turned him on his back, kneeling. 'Mac, tell nobody about this. Jim'll kill you if he hears.'

He tried, but couldn't speak. I didn't want to do that to him. He was shivering and retching. He got to his feet, swaying. I stood away and watched him. He looked at me crying. 'You scrub turkey — I've had better women than you'll ever know how to be. Real women. Not like you — half man.'

He said more, but I know he said it only because he was hurt bad.

Jim came home. His arms went around me. It was like he was dead and dragged up from the floor of the sea, and alive after all. And he emptied the boxes in front of me. Fluff and froth, they looked.

If he had emptied out parcels of diamonds I could not have been more excited. I didn't know what to say. I couldn't say pretty words. I wanted to say them but I felt shy. I've never had such pretty clothes.

'You'll look a knockout in them,' he said.

I was so pleased, but I made a disappointed face. 'You don't like me as I am.'

'All right,' he said. 'Into the fire they go.' And he scooped them up and carried them to the fireplace. But I sang out, 'No!' And he came back grinning.

'You little wild hawk,' he said. 'I bought these for a special occasion. Look!'

He pulled a little box from his pocket and there was a ring in it.

'You did mean it?'

'God Almighty, you take some convincing. Did you think I was only kidding you? Wouldn't come back? Get tied up to some dame in town?

That's what I had thought, with fear.

'Didn't think I went into town just to get a busted foot fixed did you?' He pulled me up against him, laughing. 'And, listen! we're having no honeymoon here. But, where? No damn towns!'

'No. We're goin' to have a honeymoon away from people, by

31

ourselves, the way it oughta be. Moonlight! That's where we're goin'. *Moonlight!* By ourselves. And you can wear these clothes, just for the occasion. The parson will be out next week. I was talking to him. He's fixing up everything.'

I could only hold him tight and say: 'I'm glad it's soon.'

Some people thought it was funny. They laughed and told him not to get drunk on the lashings of booze at Moonlight. They told me to be sure and get the bridal suite at the best hotel there. I felt strange in the women's clothes, but the women stared and said I looked real nice. We packed our gear and went in the flivver, rattling over the hills, into the scrub country.

We pitched our tent in Moonlight's main street, only it was green with grass now. We looked in at the old store. It was falling down. No windows, no doors. The bats camped in it. It was chinked with light, and draughts whooshed around.

This was Moonlight, and it was no more than a gully running up into the hills. Once the gully was white with tents like mushrooms, and the creek alive with men, panning and cradling. There were roaring miners in moleskins and red shirts, and gay women came from the city to play around with them for high pay.

Now there was nothing, but there was still the bloom of the plum on the hills, and the creek shining in the sun, and the ghost gums. There was the blue smoke going up from our fire, and the smell of bacon. There was the moon shining in the twilight, and the stars lighting up like blackfeller's fires.

He bit my ears and lips. He did not hurt me. I put my teeth in his brown throat but I didn't bite. I held them there on the flesh like a soft-mouthed dog.

He smelt good, the clean smell of a man. There was the white roof of the tent, and the shadow of a sapling across it. There was the night wind and the night sounds. There was a fox barking in the ranges, and the cry of a curlew and the magic of sleeping birds.

This man loved me there in the wilderness, and I loved him.

There was no one else in the world, only him and me and one blood between us. This was a great happiness and greater still because I knew then that I was a woman, too, as other women are.

We were back home only a day when someone told Jim, and he barged into Mac's hut and dragged him out. People came. Mac didn't want to fight. He kept saying: 'I was lit, Jim. I didn't know what I was doing.'

But he had to fight. He stood no chance with Jim. Jim cut him to pieces, and he fell in the dust, crumpled. Nobody moved among the onlookers, not even the women. I knelt down and lifted his head up. Blood was coming out of his mouth. Dust had gone black and thick in the blood on his face.

Jim said: 'Leave the bastard alone. Or does he mean something to you?'

I looked at Jim. 'He don't mean nothing to me, Jim, but you'd do this for a dog. You beat him. He's paid. It's finished. You're a man. Pick him up and carry him in there.'

Jim said roughly: 'Stand clear.'

And he carried Mac into his hut and helped me to wash his face and patch him, though his face was thunder and he grumbled all the time.

That night, lying in bed, Jim told me we were going away. He said there was nothing secure on the field. You worked your guts out, Jim said, and maybe you struck it good and maybe you didn't. You might starve or eat like a king. But there was too much starving in between eating like a king.

There was no point going down a hole in the earth and pulling dirt, and lying on your side with nothing in your nose but the smell of carbide, and scrabbling away with your pick watching for the gem colours until your eyes ached. And coming out and going home in the hot afternoon with nothing but a grumbling in your belly and hope for to-morrow. No point at all, Jim said, when you can be where you could work the day round and make hands and sweat pay you.

I said, 'Yes, Jim,' I looked sideways at him, I knew Mac was at the back of his decision, too.

We left in a week's time, and when we were leaving Mac came up to Jim and said: 'Let bygones be bygones, eh? So long and good luck.'

We went far out into the backwater, on horseback, packing our gear. We lived in a tent first, then we put up a log cabin. We pitsawed the timber. We trapped, and Jim took the skins to town every month. He would be away three days, but he'd go straight in and after getting the stores come straight back.

Davy came. Like a dingo whelping in the cracked rock — that's how I had him. There was no other way. I was going about the work in the house when the pains came. I went out to get Jim. I didn't think it was so near. I was in terror. Jim was across the creek felling a tree for a ford. I had to get to the top of the slope before he could see me. But I could get no farther than half-way, and I fell down there and crawled under a tree.

And that's how he came, born on the skin of the earth, on a bed of bark. Jim was holding me. He said he heard me screaming.

He was good. He knew what to do. I was full of joy, and the little baby was sleeping beside me, and I couldn't believe I had done it.

The years went by, and they were good to us. Jim took Davy out in the bush and Davy came home with rabbits and pigeons that were his own. What we got from the bush and the land we cropped was our living. We wanted for nothing, Jim educated Davy and showed me how to educate him. He told Davy he could learn a lot out of books, but not as much as he would learn when he went out in the world and met men and women and thought about things for himself.

The boy loved his father. He was a big boy with red hair that would go redder. He had big bright eyes. A nice smile. I wanted more like him, and a little girl. I did have her, and she was born dead, and I had no more children the way that one left me.

In December that year there was a great heat. The leaves curled like feathers. The creek shrank and the red dust blew from the north. The sun burned like a blue headlight in the sky.

Then Davy got sick. He was ten, and sturdy. We didn't think there was much the matter, but he got worse. He just lay in his bed, sweat-soaked. Jim wanted to get him to the doctor. But I wanted no doctor, I could pull him through.

Davy was delirious in the morning of the third day. Then he cooled and slept. He slept in the afternoon and when I went in to him at teatime there was colour in his face. He opened his eyes and looked at me. 'Mum, I'm hungry.'

I knew then that he was going to get well. I went into the kitchen. The outer yard door was open. Jim was lying on the ground just outside. I rolled him over on his back, and his eyes were open. It was getting dark. The bucket of water he had carried from the creek lay spilled on the earth.

Dead? How could he be dead?

I brought Davy a cup of milk, and he gulped it and lay back.

When I washed up, I told him, I'd come back and change his bed and make him comfortable.

Jim wasn't lying out there. In a minute he'd come in and put his arms round me and hold my breasts in his hands. He'd rub me close and put his mouth on my neck under the ear and tell me I looked good enough to eat.

Why did he die, a man like that, growing like a tree?

I couldn't go to town. I couldn't leave Davy, or take him, the way he was.

I made up his bed and waited till he was asleep. Then I closed the door. I shut the kitchen door. I got a shovel and a lantern and went down from the house. I dug a grave, and I dragged and rolled Jim down there, and on to a blanket and rolled him up in it, and put him down as gentle as I could.

The door opened and light spilled out. Davy stood in the doorway.

'Mum, where are you? What are you doing?'

I ran up to him. 'Davy, you've got to stay in bed.' I nearly said: 'Do you want to die on me too?'

'Where's Dad? Can't he come and play crib with me?'

'He's gone possuming. Now you get into bed and when I've finished I'll play crib with you Davy.'

I buried Jim. When I came in Davy was sitting up and he had the crib board on his lap. I got a chair and sat down by the bedside. Suddenly I didn't see him. I could only hear him and the surprise in his voice:

'Don't cry, Mum. Gee, Mum, you don't never cry. I'm gonna be all right. True, I am.'

I held him. I could say nothing and there was nothing to say.

I had to tell Davy his father had gone into town. I had to tell him he would be away longer than usual. Then when he was real better I had to tell him the truth. He went away in the bush and he didn't come back for hours.

When I saw him again he was sitting on the wheelbarrow looking down at the grave. He didn't talk much for a long time after. We went in to the police and they come and took Jim away, and had an inquest and buried him in the town cemetery.

We went on living there, and Davy grew up. He was tall and broad like his father, even at eighteen. And when he went to the war I stayed and looked after the place. I got letters from him, good letters, full of fun and sense. He said in one that when he came back he'd run some sheep on the place. But he didn't come back.

He wanted nothing much, only to be with me, and catch rabbits, and work. I saw him getting a woman of his own sometime, and having kids, and getting the sun for a long time.

But he won't do that now. He's a bit of me dead with his bones in the jungle swamp, him that was born under a tree in this land.

I bought a horse and caravan and I followed the roads. The roads go everywhere. I've done pea-picking and corn-pulling and fruit-packing. I was with the things I'd been with all my life. Then I came back here to Moonlight, and I will stay.

What is a life but a thing of light and shadow? You must have both to know each. I had Jim for ten years. It was into my life this man came of all lives on earth. It could have been that I had never met him. I was lucky. It's not everyone had a boy like Davy, either.

I've had no mother, except the country and the earth I've known. The seasons are like old friends coming to the door. I want no more. Lean and full years; they balance up. You go on.

I'm not going into an old folks' home. I seen a photo of those people in a home, and I seen a picture of an old ship at the bottom of the sea with fishes swimming in and out the portholes. Not much difference.

I'm going to work till I drop. Going to die with my blood hot, like my father, like Jim, like Davy. Fall down on the earth and die.

A WOMAN OF THE COUNTRY

I needed no encouragement.

He took me into the cool dining room, full of morning shadows and the smell of floor polish. I put my hat under the chair and sat at the table, and he went out into the kitchen. I looked at all the tables with the white cloths on them and the empty chairs around them, and I was glad that breakfast was well over, and there were no diners about. I was glad I was on my own.

I saw the girl come to the kitchen door leading to the dining room and look briefly at me. He was explaining. I felt a sudden embarassing humiliation when I saw her. I thought I'd get my hat and go out there. But I didn't. I guess I didn't know how.

The girl came in from the kitchen with cold meat on a plate, and bread and butter. I just looked at her. Her face was solemn. Then I said: Hello. She didn't answer, but put the things down, and set my knife and fork.

I felt it inside me: a warm feeling for the kindness of the publican and a resentment against his charity. It was the look in the girl's eyes that did that, and her silence that seemed reproachful.

I was no beggar, I wanted to tell her that. I wanted to tell her

38

that he spoke to me outside, off his own bat, and asked me where I was making. And I said: I'm waiting to go out with a bloke in a car to a shed this afternoon. And he said: Are you holding all right? And I said: I'm okay, but I'll be better when I eat. And he said: Have a feed on me; I battled, too. And so here I am.

I wanted to say those things to get the indifferent look off her face; to make her smile at me.

She had such long eyelashes; like a foal's.

I watched her go away, and I didn't start eating because I knew she'd be back with the pot of tea. I waited until she came and went, and then the mutton on my plate vanished. I ate it hard like a dog. When I felt eyes on me I looked up suddenly towards the kitchen door. I saw a shadow flit away, and there was heat in my face.

She came again, and said: 'Any more?'

I said: 'Is it all right?'

'Why not?'

'Thanks,' I said. 'It's good of you.'

She didn't look at me. She said, as she whipped the plate up: 'Boss said to give you all you wanted. Don't thank me.'

There was a sullen coldness in her voice. She looked down on me. She thought I was a loafer and a bum, and she made me feel it. She wanted to make me feel it. It made me angry. I looked at her when she came back, watching for the apology in her eyes, but it wasn't there. There was no shame for her attitude.

Suddenly I didn't care. I wanted her to stay there; to sit down and talk to me while I looked at her with her long-lashed eyes and her young neck and the sheen on her black hair. But she went back to the kitchen, and I felt disappointed and discontented; and when I finished I contrived to clink the cup on the saucer to attract her, but she didn't come back. And I went out.

The publican was in the bar: 'How's that feel?' he said.

'Feels good. Thanks. Where's the park from here?'

'Coupla hundred yards up. Why?'

'Think I'll go and have a bit of a lay-off.'

He was all right, I thought. He wouldn't hear of that. He let me go up and sleep in a room off the balcony. I lay down on the cool bed, and stared at the ceiling, and the wallpaper, and the jug with the blue flowers on it on the marble wash-stand.

I wish I had the taming of you. I'd tame you. I'd make you look up to me as the god that filled your world, the hunter of your food, and the hero of your love-bed. You wouldn't toss your head at me in scorn, or seal your smile away out of contempt.

I fell asleep thinking of her, and I slept long and deep. When I woke the spring was back in me. Travelling all night in the back of that lorry from the other town had been pretty wearying. But now I felt good. I saw her again when I was going down the back stairs; and, somehow, I didn't want to meet her, but it was too late to return, and I knew she would see my weakness if I did. She was in the yard taking clothes off the clothes-line.

I thought I'd better say something, and I said: 'It's a bonzer day.' And I gave her a smile.

She went on gathering the clothes into the basket without a word.

I went on talking, to let her think I hadn't noticed the snub: 'It's a nice little town, this. I wouldn't mind living here. Maybe I will, after the shed cuts out. For a while, anyway. I'll have a pretty fair cheque, and I might as well bust it up here as anywhere else.'

She gave me a short, piercing look, almost savage in its scorn, picked up the basket and walked off; leaving me standing there, foolish and puzzled, wishing I hadn't spoken.

That afternoon I went out to the shed and bunked up with Andy Craven. In the daytime, when I was at the wool-table, with the fleeces coming down, being skirted and rolled and passed to the classer, it was all right. We were busy; and there was the noise of the machinery. It lulled your mind. But at night it was hard. I lay on my bunk and tried to read magazines.

A WOMAN OF THE COUNTRY

I heard the men laughing and yarning out around the camp-
fire, and some of them over in the cookhouse, listening to
Pasty Tommy, the cook from the Big Smoke. He was a good
entertainer. When it got too disturbing for me, I picked up my
pannikin and went over for a mug of coffee, and a listen, and
maybe I had a yarn with the presser, or the penner-up, or one
of the shearers.

But she was there all the time.

Then I went back to my room. Old Andy might want me to
rub him down if his backache was bad, or talk me into washing
his greasy duds on Saturday afternoon, or Sunday, for a few
bob; or tell about the horses who'd romped home for him, or
the lottery tickets he had taken and never won a cracker, until
he fell asleep with his mouth open and his face sagging in a
way that somehow made me feel a great sadness for the long
hard years of work behind him.

I put the light out, but I couldn't sleep. I kept thinking of
her. In the end I got up and went out to the camp-fire's few
coals, and threw a stick or two on, and sat there with my palms
over the blaze. I didn't feel angry with her any more. I didn't
want to tame her. I just wanted to see her. She was good. She
was beautiful. There was nothing in the world to match her. I
had never come across anyone like her before, and she had to
be for me. I wanted to see her and her long eyelashes.

Underneath that coldness she must have felt something for
me. It was too pointed. I told myself she was putting on a
front, as many of them do. She'd come round. Maybe I
shouldn't have said that about busting up the cheque, though.
Maybe I should have given her the idea I was thrifty, which I
am; thrifty enough. It might have made some difference to her
if I had told her that.

You could knock the stars out of the sky with a stick, they
were so big and near. But when I looked at them, I thought of
the things that men said were written in them for men. And I
wondered what was written there for me. The blackness
behind them was like her hair.

I was glad when Saturday came. I went in and I paid the

41

publican for the feed he'd given me. He didn't want it, but I pressed it on him, so I could show him I had some principle, and so I could ask him a question. I asked him: 'Where is that girl from the kitchen? She was nice to me. I'd like to give her something, a box of chocolates, or something.'

He said: 'Merle?'

I nodded, though I didn't know her name was Merle.

He said: 'Merle's off for the week-end; won't be back till Monday.'

'Oh, I see,' I said.

'Would you like me to pass your present on?'

'No — no, it's all right. I'll be in again next week.'

I went out. The town held nothing for me. Only a lot of cockies in for the week-end, and girls arm-in-arming it up and down the street, and looking for catches, and the catches in hooped ties and Saturday-cleaned shoes not being slow to be caught.

I bought some pies, and sauntered down to the park. Another week! God, it would seem like a year. I left the park and walked up and down the street, looking in the windows, hanging about, wishing I was back at the shed, and knowing how much worse it would be there.

Then I thought it mightn't be such a bad idea after all to leave a present for her with the publican. It would help to break the ice for me; it would be easier to see her next week. That bucked me up a lot. I bought what I wanted and went back to the publican.

'Who do I say it's from?' he asked. 'What name?'

'It's all fixed up,' I told him. 'I put a little note inside.'

'All right, lad; I'll see she gets it okay.'

'Thanks very much.'

I was going out when he called me back. 'Say,' he said, looking straight at me, 'you're not trying to do a line with Merle by any chance, are you?'

'No,' I said. 'No. I just wanted to give her a little something for her kindness, that's all. I had —'

'I was just going to say, I don't think you'd do much good for yourself. I think you'd be wasting your time. She's got some — well, some funny ideas, Merle. However,' he chucked my arm, and grinned, 'that won't worry you if you're not making a pitch for her.'

'No, no, that won't worry me,' I tossed off, and went out.

But I was curious and worried about what he said. Funny ideas? What sort of funny ideas? I felt he had been going to tell me. Maybe he would have if I'd told him I was interested in her. I don't know why I made out I wasn't. It just came into my head to say what I did. I was annoyed at his penetrativeness and his questions.

But after a while I began to think warmly of her again, and the impression my gift would make on her, and I didn't think of anything else. Cheerfully, I went to the pictures, sitting down the front, and laughing with everyone else at the antics of the Marx Brothers. After the show I helped Teddy Fowler to round up the boys, and we all went back to the shed singing the 'Hag's Lament' and 'Little Nelly Kelly' while Teddy kept his bus on the road by luck only. At the shed they swarmed into Mick Doolan the presser's room, turning on a booze party and filling it with smoke and song and the rumble of bottles, while cursing protests came in relays from the huts.

I lay on my bunk, thinking of Merle.

On Sunday I washed my own and all Andy's clothes, and Andy wanted to know whether I'd consider giving him my hand in marriage. I thought of her all day, excitedly. She might write me a letter. She might even come out, as visitors often did from the town; girls who stood on the board and made the shearers show off something wicked, and blokes who'd never seen a sheep shorn in their lives.

I was so sure I'd get a letter on Tuesday that it was shock of disappointment when I didn't. I couldn't do my work right. The classer chipped me a couple of times during the afternoon. And that night Andy nearly drove me crazy with his yabber. I got away from him and went for a walk. I needed the silence.

I wish she could have heard what I was thinking.

Think of me, will you, think of me and something of me.
I've got no one. I never had anyone since I left the orphanage.
I haven't come across anyone like you before, and there isn't
anyone. I've found you now. What's wrong with me? I'm
young. I'm only twenty. I'm strong and healthy and clean, I've
knocked around, living a hard life. I can do anything, and I'm
not afraid of anything. Why don't you come out and ask for
me? You don't know what happiness that would give me. Ask
for me, and make it easy for me to know you and be friends.
Tell me you'd like to go to the pictures with me. Give me a
chance to let you understand me. So that you want me, and
will tell me that you'll think of me always; and the sun is gone
out like a fire when I am not there where you are, just as it is
when you are not here with me.

I hardly slept that night, hoping for some word from her in
the morning. I was up early, and was over in the cookhouse
talking with the cook while he got the breakfast ready. I didn't
know impatience could affect a man's nerves so much until
that day. Smoko passed, and dinner, and there was still no sign
of the mailman.

He came during the three o'clock smoko; and I felt the
palms of my hands sweating while Jim Burgess, the rep,
handed out the mail. I saw him coming across the wool-room
towards me, looking down at a parcel in his hand. He gave it to
me, and looked at the address on the next letter.

I tore the string and paper off; and felt a sort of sickness in
the pit of the stomach. I opened the box. All the fellows sitting
about me on the bales stared with interest.

'Chocolates! Who's sending you chocolates, Sammy?'

'Gord, don't tell me Sammy's got a girl!'

'What's her name, Sammy? Have to give us a knockdown
sometime.'

'Did she make 'em herself?'

'Let's try one, Sammy.'

They laughed and went on chaffing me. What made it worse:
she had sent my note back, too. There was nothing else. Just

the chocolates and the note. I felt a wild rage come up in me, and I heard them laughing still and cracking jokes; and I only remember that the sound cut off suddenly when I shouted something and threw the chocolates among them and told them to shut their mouths.

When I could see them they were staring at me in surprise; and then telling me I didn't want to be thin-skinned, and I had to learn to take a joke, and no offence was meant.

I didn't blame them. They didn't know.

I didn't want any tea that evening. I couldn't get her out of my mind. I wanted to take her and beat her. But it was only rage. I knew I loved her, and couldn't hurt her.

Someone shouted that Teddy Fowler was going for a spin into town. I found Teddy and asked him if I could come. I didn't bother to dress up; just put on my overcoat over my working clothes. We hit the town about eight, and I went straight to the hotel.

The yardman told me Merle's room was off the balcony, and he gave me the number and I went up there and knocked on the door. She opened it wide, and I saw that she was dressed to go out. There was a smile on her face, but it vanished so swiftly when she saw who I was that I hardly had time to notice it. And her expression turned with the same swiftness to flashing fury.

'Listen, if you don't stop hounding me, by God I'll get the police on to you!'

I started to say something, but she slammed the door in my face. I stood there for a minute, inflamed, wanting to kick the door in, and tell her what I thought of her. But I thought how useless that would be. I went down the stairs, and around the back of the pub into the parlor. The publican seemed a little surprised to see me.

'Can I have a bottie?' I asked him.

He shook his head: 'I'm sorry. You know the law.'

'Those chocolates you gave her for me — she sent them back.'

'Merle?'

45

'What's up with her? What's wrong with me? You'd think I was poison. You'd think I'd done something to her.' I looked at him. 'Can you tell me why she should treat me like a dog?'

'Listen, son, I've seen a lot of the world; you haven't. You're too young. But you know this much: you know how people sometimes get the idea that they're better than you are? How they put themselves above you, and would no more think of associating themselves with you than they would with a leper. They're always drawing a line, for some reason or another, selecting and casting out. You know that well enough, don't you?'

'I know it all right,' I said. 'But she — she's not like that, is she?'

'She's a lot like that.'

'But how — why?'

I looked wildly at him. He took my arm: 'Listen,' he said, 'you forget her. Just go back to your job and forget all about her. There are plenty of girls as nice as Merle, and nicer, who'd think the sun shone out of you. Merle's no good to you. You'll only give yourself a lot of unnecessary unhappiness if you keep on trying to get somewhere with her. Do as I say and you won't be sorry.'

He came down the hall to the back door with me, and I went on out through the yard. I puzzled over his words and only became more confused. In the car going back they asked me why I was so quiet. I told them I had toothache.

I stuck it out through Thursday and Friday, and when Saturday came I was desperate. I couldn't get into town fast enough. I went around into the pub yard and knocked at the kitchen door. The fat woman-cook came and said: 'Well, what can I do for you?'

'Is Merle there?'

'I'll see,' she said.

'Tell her it's important.'

I wet my lips, and waited for the light footfalls, but only the heavy ones returned, and the cook said with her mouth crimped up: 'Merle doesn't want to see you.'

'Does she know who it is that's here?'

'I told her.'

'And she won't see me?'

'That's what she said.'

'But why? It's only for a minute or two. Did you tell her it was . . .'

She said: 'Look, I'm not going to argue with you. She doesn't want to see you.' She slapped the gauze door shut and left me standing there.

I went away slowly, angrily, and sat down on the kerb, and wondered and felt sick with disappointment and frustration. I thought of her slim body, and her youth, and everything about her; and she was so far away, so unattainable. I didn't know what I could do to show her what I thought of her. I couldn't be beaten. It couldn't be the end. That wasn't bearable.

I felt myself fighting with rage against the thought, and I felt the primitive urge to tame her. I thought I'd hang about and hope to see her. And I did. It was later in the afternoon, and the pub was full of men, spilling out into groups talking in the yard.

When I saw her come out and cross to the line, I went forward and said straight: 'What's the matter with you? You must get a great kick out of insulting and hurting people. I'd like to know why you've got it in for me.'

'Don't talk to me,' she snapped.

I looked at her: 'Think yourself too good for me — is that it? Why are you too good for me? You're a woman of the country, as I'm a man. We're the same; in one class. Where do you get off thinking you're too good for me?'

'Don't you call me a woman of the country!' she shrieked, and her eyes flashed fiercely.

I don't know how it happened, but some one must have tipped the man off; for he came across the yard, two others with him, and he said: 'What's up with you, mug?'

'Nothing's up with me,' I said.

'Not much!' the girl sneered.

Then this white man hit me in the mouth, and I fell down,

and shook my head, and saw the scarlet blood fall on my hands. I was too shocked to get up straightaway.

'Like his damn cheek!' the girl snorted. 'Trying to make up to me.'

I heard the feet all round, stamping over the gravel, and saw the legs surrounding, and I got up, and hit him. And kept hitting him till my knuckles skinned on his teeth, and he fell down. And I heard the girl screeching. And then his cobbers hoed into me, and I couldn't handle two men, and none in the crowd offered to help me until it was too late. I don't remember much more, but when I woke I was propped against the lavatory wall, and there were two men on their haunches looking at me, and a crowd behind them.

One said: 'How you feel now, Darky?'

I was chewing on blood, and I had to tilt my face to see the other man when he spoke, because I could only see out of one eye. This man said: 'That piece is Rusty Bennett's girl, half-caste and all as she is. You don't want to muck about with her. Rusty'll kill you.'

'And she'll be barracking for him,' said the other man.

Then I saw the publican stoop down. He held a glass of water to my lips, and he was talking. His face was strained and distressed and he was talking.

I saw their faces suddenly change, and, because I was crying, I yelled at them to get away and leave me alone, to get away to hell and leave me alone; leave me alone, leave me alone! And I staggered out of that place; and felt ashamed of making a sobbing sound, but it was working some of the bitterness and treachery and hate and loneliness out of my heart, so I let it keep on as I found the quiet street and the park.

But I kept hearing the words of the publican. They kept splitting and crashing in my mind:

She resented you making up to her as much as if she were a white woman. She doesn't want to be a wake-up to her own

48

skin, and, tough as it is, son, you're the sort that won't let her forget it.

The words, the words, and the hatred and savagery of their meaning.

And I didn't see the bitter dusk coming down on me. I only knew that I was walking back, out along that still road to the shed, to get my things together and clear out.

HUNTER OF DRAGONFLIES

*H*o Van Thi, in the sad method of age, went a little way past the trucks and stopped to bring the air into his lungs. He was in rags. The stick helped him to get along. He looked at the trucks, each marked with a red cross; he saw the tents and the men lying about; men with bandages on them, and, like dogs, panting in the shade.

He went up to the door of the hospital. A tall shadow fell straight on him, arched like a tree that has long grown against the wind. Four other shadows fell and cooled him. He looked at all the faces, and they looked at his face, broken in wrinkles. They saw the sewn-up mouth, and the diamond-shaped eyes glazed with grape blue.

'Yes, old man?'

'I have come to see Pham Chanh Ky. He is here?'

'We will have to see.'

'They told me,' said the old man. 'A friend. By chance it was.'

'Are you a relative?'

'His grandfather.'

'Wait here.'

The old man sat down. The men said to him: 'You will know soon.'

They were young fellows. There was hard bitterness in their eyes, a determined ruthlessness. But they laughed and chiacked as they looked at him. They did it from good nature, from gladness, for they reverenced age. It was just because they could see his nervousness, his eagerness, the little ways he showed his expected delight.

The old man thought of the boy, his grandson.

He thought of him in the garden, chasing after the dragonflies. He could see the flashing tint of the rainbow in their wings as they darted out beyond the low wall that hemmed the boy in. The boy only turned away laughing in the zest of life and play. He sat down now, a hot flame in his face, the color of a pear, and prattled. His eyes shone. The old man thought of how they talked, while the fountain chirruped, and the birds sang and flittered in the leaning branches, heavy with blue-powdered plums.

'How long will it take to grow a white beard like yours, grandfather?'

'Seventy years it will take you, my son.'

'And can I have no hair on my head soon?'

'That is for wisdom and nature to decide.'

'I wish I was more than seven.'

'You will be. You will be.'

Then, with a loud cry, he was off again after the darting dragonfly.

The orderly came back.

'Yes,' he said. 'He is here, old man, but you cannot see him.'

'I must. I must.'

'He is being operated on. You must wait.'

'I will wait,' said Ho Van Thi.

A young Vietnamese lit a cigarette, wiped the sweat away from under his cap.

'A good soldier, Pham Chanh Ky,' he said. 'He fought bravely last night. The life of an officer is owed to him. He fought like a demon. You can be proud of him.'

The old man made no response at all.

The soldier drew hard on his cigarette.

Another said: 'You know that fellow, Pham Chanh Ky, do you?'

'We have fought together now a good while.'

'They tell me he once had great riches.'

'He was the son of a merchant.' The man blew out the smoke.

'Yes, they were well off. His grandfather there, he knows. Eh, old man?'

The old man looked in the dust and said nothing. He was thinking of the boy in the garden.

'You have only to look at him to see what hard times came upon the family.'

'These things happen.'

'It's buried in the past. The brutes killed the mother. The father. They took everything, property, house, land. Gone forever.'

'That's this business for you,' the other said.

'All of them — torn apart, lost to each other.'

'What did Pham do?'

'What could he do? A waif running wild like all the others. He ended up in a village in the mountains, he told me. At thirteen he was helping the partisans. At seventeen he was among us.'

'He's been through it then.'

The soldier nodded. 'All the way, years of it. He's tramped in blood all right. I suppose he would be a merchant now, like his father, only for the war.'

'And I suppose,' said the other; 'I suppose the old man there hasn't seen his grandson for a long time now.'

The soldier looked at the old man.

'Pham never mentioned him to me. I suppose he thought he was dead. How long, old man? Eh, how long?'

Ho Van Thi did not speak. How did he know how long since he had seen the boy? Eight, nine, ten years — how did he know? All he knew was that the memory was as vivid as yesterday. He saw him there in the garden at his favorite pastime, chasing the dragonfly. He saw him blowing on the lip of a bottle and the bottle whistling; his mother laughing at him, her earrings bobbing like little green cucumbers; he remembered how he laughed when his father caught him and tickled his ribs. Plainly he saw him under the blue sky, in the garden, and the serenity there was like a dream.

The old man saw the orderly come out again, and he went up to him.

'Can I see Pham Chanh Ky now?'

'He cannot see you, old man.'

'Where is he?'

'They will fetch him out in a moment.'

Four men brought the figure out on a stretcher. Old Ho stopped them. He lifted the blanket from the face.

What he saw was a stranger, a face that belonged to a thousand other soldiers he had seen. His lips trembled. He stared, while disappointment surged and built in him: looking for dark red lips and eyes shining like black water; for a skin glossy as a persimmon; for a vitality that showed mischief, innocence, laughter. But he saw only a mask, hard and dust-coloured, the mouth open, teeth protruding over blistered lips, and a glassy strip of brown eye under the lid.

The old man's hands shook. He put the blanket back gently and said nothing.

A man said: 'You are his grandfather. He has no one else. Are there any words you would like on his grave?'

Ho Van Thi only stared.

'Say: Here lies a true soldier,' offered one man.

'Or; He died that we might live,' said another.

'He knew blood and guts,' put in a third. 'What about: He killed hundreds of the devils?'

They paused.

'Well, what shall it be, old man?'

Ho did not answer; only stared and nodded his head in a dazed feeble way. Then he heard no voices, saw no shadows. He looked up in a startled awareness. He saw the soldiers a good way off, and he went slowly towards them.

They had nearly finished their task, and he waited until they had gone. Then he stood before the rough board headstone; and because he did not know the man he had seen, but only remembered a boy in a garden, he scratched on the mound with his stick the question: 'Where is he today — that brave hunter of dragonflies?'

ONE TOO MANY

I didn't get to sleep for a long time. I heard Duggie snoring, then Tookley, but I couldn't be sure whether Tookley was on the level. I slept because I couldn't keep the sleep off any longer. At daylight I woke. Tookley had the fire going, the blue smoke curling out of the dewy kindling. He had bacon in a pan: it was just buckling and going transparent and the smell starting from it.

'Morning,' he said, as I jumped up and gave Duggie a push. He woke with a quick, startled look on his face, eyes bloodshot. I knew then that he had been doing a lot of thinking during the night. And I thought: He's the one who was putting on the snoring.

He went down to the creek for a wash.

'Listen, Duggie,' I said. 'That big cow gives me the creeps. What's his caper?'

'I dunno,' Duggie said. 'But don't let's get stirred up about it yet. We'll wipe him soon as we can.'

He was big enough to eat an elephant, one gulp, this Tookley. And he looked like something that had just come down out of a cave, slapped on some dusty old mokker, and sat on the log hunched over the tin plate on his knees and eating with his fingers.

'That's the last of me tucker,' he said. 'I cooked it all. You boys help yourselves.'

Duggie, with the clear eyes like honey and the half-smile on his face, nodded: 'We got a bit of beef and damper, mate. We're right.'

Tookley picked up the pan and slapped a hunk of bacon on to each of our plates. 'Mates share and share alike,' he said gruffly.

'Okay,' I said. 'I'm easy.'

We ate in silence. Then I caught Duggie looking at his nap on the ground, and followed his gaze. I couldn't see anything wrong, but I didn't miss the narrowing of his eyes. Then he became the palavery little man again: 'Where you heading, mate?'

'Where're you?' Tookley said.

'Gurley.'

'Same here,' nodded Tookley. 'Know the publican there. We'll be right for a real spread tonight.'

Duggie looked at me under his eyebrows. I shrugged. What could he do? Tookley told us to give him our things and he'd wash 'em down at the creek. When he was out of earshot, Duggie snarled grimly: 'That big bludger's been at my gear.'

'What makes you think that?'

'When we were away having a wash, it must have been. That flour bag with my few private things in it was under my pillow.' He pointed to his rolled-up coat. 'It was sticking out when we came back.'

'He couldn't of had time.'

'To pinch anything, no. But he was at it. How's your swag?'

'Looks okay.' I had my stuff in a sugar bag. The neck was still tied. 'But I don't like the big sod, Duggie. He's up to no good.'

'Watch him, that's all. We'll get rid of him just as soon as we can.'

We hit the road and Tookley did most of the talking. He reckoned he'd carried his swag all over Australia, and had been on the track since he was a kid. Except for the years when he did time. Duggie looked at him when he said that, but it didn't raise any pimples on me. Lots of silly mugs like to say they've done time. It proves them toughies, battlers who've been around, they think. Get to the truth of it, and you'll find most of these skite-peddlers have been lumbered for chiselling the busman, lifting their mate's overcoat or scoring over some silly biddy.

'I like mates,' Tookley said. 'Some jokers go round on their paddy, but I reckon that does things to a man. He needs a cobber. I can see you two blokes are great mates.'

'Yeah, me and Duggie hit it off all right,' I said.

'A man knows when he's got a good mate,' Duggie put in.

'How long you been together?'

''Bout a week,' Duggie said. 'Me and Jimmy palled up in Moree — what is it, Jimmy — six, seven days ago?'

'That's right,' I said.

We said nothing about it being in a police line-up.

'Well, there you are,' said Tookley. 'That shows you, don't it? I had a cobber once. Me and him went everywhere. Then a woman grabbed him, and it was like they cut my arm off, or part of my brain out. I've never forgotten that bloke for what he did to me. I hope he fries in hell. And his missus with him.'

Duggie and I looked at each other, but said nothing. The big fellow stepped out ahead of us, swinging along. You could see how tall and thick he was. He made nearly two of Duggie and me, and we weren't runts. Duggie was chunky, solid. I used to fight welterweight.

After a while Tookley said to me: 'Let's carry your swag for a spell. You look all in.'

'Who? Me?' I said. 'Like hell I'm all in.'

'Come on,' said Tookley, with a touch of bounce in his voice.

'She's right,' I said, a bit firmer. 'I carry me own swag. Think a man's a quean?'

Duggie laughed, trying, I thought, to make sure the big man saw it as a joke. He was a dual personality, this Duggie. Quiet, nice as pie to the big feller, and yet inside him distrustful, resentful.

We sauntered into the sleepy town about four. We went up to the pub, parched. Tookley said we'd be right and we were letting it go at that. There were a couple of loungers in the bar, and an old man sitting on a form, dozing, with his hands clasped on the head of an upright walking stick.

Tookley said to the barman. 'Where's the boss, Richards?'

'Richards? He's not the boss here. Not now.'

'Since when?'

'Since a year ago,' the barman said.

'Who's running the place now?'

'Ed Davidson.'

Duggie shrugged: 'Well, that stumps us.'

Tookley said: 'No, it don't — by hell. How about it, barman? We're flat, but we'll fix it up when we come good.'

'I'm sorry, mate. I can't without the boss's okay, and he ain't here.'

'Come on, be a sport — you can stretch a point.'

The barman shook his head, full of ease, slopping over the counter with a cloth in a fat, lazy way.

Tookley looked nasty. 'You're no country man,' he snapped.

'Born and bred here.'

'Bulldust. From the Smoke, you, if ever I seen a cityite.'

'Take it or leave it, chum. Why should I argue with Mother Murphy's crystal ball?'

'Smart with the talk — just like the city whacker.' Tookley leant over the bar. 'You louse. It's only a louse who'd knock a man back for a drink on a day like this. But you'll learn.'

'I can see,' said the barman, with a cool flash of anger, 'plenty have told you what you can go and do. Well, put me down at the top of the list.'

He sidled away.

Tookley said to us: 'You two wait here. If I can't rake up a few bob I'll give the game away. Just hang on. I won't be long.'

When he went out, Duggie turned to me: 'Now's our chance to skip. Give him the brush-off.'

ONE TOO MANY

'Damn him!' I said. 'I got money, but I wasn't letting on to him.'

Duggie looked surprised.

'Well, ain't you the dark horse?' he said, licking his lips with pleasure.

'The tail end of my rabbit cheque. Not much — but I wasn't going to flash it in front of that mug.'

Duggie nodded. I had been putting out a few bob, same as he had, for tucker and weed, but we'd been getting along mainly on handouts. Duggie was all right. He was skinned, I had no intention of holding out on him.

I called the barman, told him to stand up a couple, and shot the ten-bob note across the counter. He just looked his query and answered it in his mind. He pulled the beers. He leaned on the counter: 'Thought you was cobbers with that big yob.'

'Well, we're not,' I said.

'Listen,' Duggie said, putting down his empty glass at the same time as me. 'That bloke's a bit of a bat. Ugly phiz, big head, big mouth full of gab — we don't know him from Adam, but we're stuck with him.'

'How long's he been with you?'

'Since yesty,' Duggie said. 'Me and Jimmy here are walking along an hour before camping time when this cow — well, he's sitting on his swag by the roadside. We think he's waiting for a ride. We just get to talking a bit, you know, like you do with anybody. Then we move off, and, damn me if he don't start to foot it along with us.'

'Like a stray dog,' the barman nodded comprehendingly with a side grin and placed the beers in front of us.

'Stray dog?' Duggie said. 'You can get rid of a stray dog, but what do you do with a bit of bloody flypaper?'

'Which way'd you come?'

'Moree. We're making down to Manila.'

The barman wiped the slops up. 'Crook business that murder they had in Limben. S'pose you heard a lot about it on your way through?'

Duggie looked at me, winked, and I looked at the barman:

59

'No, didn't even know there was one. What happened?'

'Some bloke broke into the Brady homestead, ratted the place of jewellery and notes, and shot the old housekeeper and the gardener dead. They were the only ones there.'

'Go on?'

'Nobody knew till next day when a farmer named McKillop made a call and discovered the business. The Bradys were all away at the Wallangarra show. Dirty lowdown crime. Two old people. Nice folks, too. I seen 'em plenty times.'

'When'd this happen?' Duggie asked.

'Oh, must be ten or twelve days ago now. Fill 'em up again?'

'That's the idea,' I said.

Duggie turned to me: 'Just shows you, Jimmy, what goes on and you don't know anything about it.'

'This one might trip 'em up — police, I mean,' said the barman.

'They don't look like getting a clue; had the dees up from Sydney, too. Funny you heard nothing.'

'What talks out there on the road?' I asked. We haven't seen a paper for a month or more, eh, Duggie?'

'That's right, mate.'

Why tell him we were among those roped in for questioning? They roped in everybody — even the dogs.

The barman went off to serve a couple who idled in. Duggie said we had to get rid of Tookley. The few quick beers made him a little careless, and he said: 'I'm a bit windy of him, Jimmy, and so are you, ain't you?'

'He's not a bloke I'd like to tangle with,' I said.

'I dunno what to do, mate?'

'Christ,' I said. 'It's a free country. You can pick your own company. If you don't want a mug tagging along you've got every right to wipe him.'

'Sure, but how?' Like I said, do it the hard way and how does he come back at you? He's as mad as a hatter. The sort that might make a mess of a man with a broken bottle, or come the knife-work or something, if he was put out.'

'There must be a way,' I said. 'He's after something, and it's not healthy the way I see it.'

Then Duggie slapped his thigh: 'Listen I got an idea. What's wrong with getting him pinched?'

'Pinched? I don't catch on.'

'This murder,' Duggie said.

'You're not making sense, mate.'

'Listen,' Duggie said. 'One of us rings up the copshop, says something like this: You're looking for the Limben murderer. Here's a tip. Why don't you have a word with a man named Tookley. He's right in this town now.' Duggie grinned at me: 'They grab Tookley for questioning and we scarper out of here.'

'Wait a minute — you mean an anonymous phone call?'

'That's it.'

'But everybody that seen us knows all three of us came into this town together. If Tookley was nabbed, it's on the cards they'd take us along, too. And, hell, we don't want that trouble. See?'

Duggie though for a moment; then he nodded: 'Yeah, maybe you're right.'

'Shut up, here he comes.'

Tookley had a big grin on his face. In his hand was a wad of notes. We gaped at it. He slapped it down on the bar. There must have been fifteen or twenty greenskins. 'How's my touch?' he said.

I looked at him suspiciously. Where could he have got all that dough? You couldn't tell me he borrowed it. Duggie met my gaze, and you could see his thoughts flipping over. Bunging on the arrogance, Tookley called the barman, slipped a quid from the bank, and said:

'There's your cue, louse. Start pulling those beers.'

We had half a dozen. Then we went to the Greek's for a feed. I couldn't get over Tookley coming by all that oscar. Maybe he hadn't. Maybe he'd had it all along. What was his game?

As the Greek put the ham and eggs down in front of us,

Duggie said, winking at me: 'Well, Jimmy, it's been pretty good. I'm sorry we're splitting up.'

Tookley came in: 'Did you say splitting up?'

'Yeah. Jimmy's decided to make out Walgett way. I'm sticking to Manila. Looks like you'll be going another way, too, eh?'

Tookley looked taken aback. I was beginning to cotton on. He couldn't tag along with both of us.

'Well, that's a bit of a cow,' Tookley said. 'But I reckon I'll just have to make up me mind which one of you I like best. Well, I think I'll stick with Jimmy here. No offence meant, Duggie.'

Well, strike me dead, I had to laugh. I just threw my head back and laughed. There was no getting rid of this prickly pear. Duggie joined me. But Tookley didn't see the joke. He just looked at us enquiringly. I put my head down and bogged in. I was thinking hard, and beginning to get a bit resentful towards Duggie. He had thrown the whole sixteen stone baby in my lap. He was free. I had the job of getting rid of Tookley.

Tookley, when he finished his meal, went over to the counter for cigarettes.

'Well, this is nice,' I told Duggie.

'I was only trying,' he said. 'I never thought for a minute that he . . .'

'And why'd he pick me instead of you? I've given him no encouragement.'

'What do we do now?' Duggie said.

I was thinking. Anger was getting hold of me. Duggie went on: 'Say we go through with it, Jimmy — just a temporary split? You give him the slip, and we'll meet somewhere.'

'Listen, Duggie,' I said, 'I've had this. It's too bloody silly for words. I'm not messing about any longer. We're getting out of here. Tonight.'

'Together?'

'Yeah, together.'

'Do me, son,' Duggie said. 'But how?'

I glanced across at Tookley. He was chiacking the Greek's wife. She had the same face as Mona Lisa, and about the same expression, but Tookley was trying hard to change it. 'A man could tell him straight where to get off,' I said. 'But listen, I've got another idea and I think it'll be less trouble. That 4.15 goods from Moree — she'll be through here in about fifteen or twenty minutes. She'll take us south. In a few minutes I'll get up and go out. Follow?'

'Yeah.'

'I'll leave you here. Right?'

'Right.'

'Soon as we go out, me and Tookley, you hotfoot it over there to the yards and wait for me near the goods-shed.'

'What about your swag?'

'You take that, because I might be running.'

'I got you,' Duggie said.

'Let me play the cards; you just watch the cues.'

Tookley returned and handed out the cigarettes. I didn't let on to him how impatient I was getting. I said: 'Well, Took, I don't know about you, but I could do that feed again. So could Duggie here.'

'Well, we'll have it,' boomed Tookley. 'I got plenty chips. Hey, boss'

'No, wait a minute, wait a minute.' I said. 'Not yet. I just thought of something. I don't see why we shouldn't have a good sleep with feathers on the bed tonight. That publican's got three beds on the verandah. I found out today. I'm going to put the acid on him.'

'Why crawl?' said Tookley. 'We can pay.'

'No, we don't want to come the bludge on you. I . . .'

'No bludge. We're mates.'

'Yeah, and this is my way of doing my bit. The drinks were on you, the feed was on you; this is on me. I like to pull my weight, too.'

'Okay,' Tookley said, pleased, as I thought he would be. 'I like your form, Jimmy.'

I stood up: 'That barman told me his boss'd be there between half past seven and eight. He was going to a dance later. So I better get going if I want to catch him. How about coming along for the walk, Duggie?'

'Who, me? God, I couldn't walk another yard, Jim.' Duggie made it look real good. 'Took'll go with you.' He stretched and groaned with relaxation.

'Ah, you're cracking up,' I told him with a grin. 'What do you say, Took, or are your varicose veins playing up, too?'

Tookley was in it, and I made for the door. Tookley lingered, laughing and exchanging banter with Duggie. Then he was in step with me.

I told Tookley to wait for me outside the pub, as this was my pigeon and I wanted to do it alone. He didn't say a word, just nodded easily. I should have smelled a rat then.

I went straight through to the office, into a side passage that brought me to a door leading out to the backyard. There were still a few after-hours drinkers in the bar. I pelted across the yard, scaled the fence, and went around by a side street into another that touched on the east end of the railway yards.

Duggie was waiting for me at the goods shed. We said nothing, but ran up on the blind side of the rattler, threw our swags into an open truck and climbed up. Duggie wanted to know the story, but I told him it would keep. All I said was: 'The big mug is still waiting outside the pub. You can kiss Tookley goodbye.'

The train was under way ten minutes when something shuffled in a loosely-rolled tarp at one end of the truck. A figure scrambled out and started to crawl towards us. It stopped halfway, and a match flared and the figure lit a cigarette in its mouth.

'Strike me dead!' cried Duggie. 'It's Tookley!'

Tookley stood up and so did I. I couldn't fathom it, but I wasn't trying to. All I knew was that I'd had this crackpot once and for all. I pulled the automatic from inside my coat and told him straight: 'Get off!'

'Now cut that out, Jimmy,' Tookley said, calm.

'Come on, jump!'

Duggie might have been surprised to know I had a gun, and it might have put the sharp notes in his voice: 'Take it easy, Jimmy. You don't want that thing to go off. Give him a chance. Wait till we hit the upgrade.'

'Get off now, Tookley. You big bastard, I'm not kidding!'

I felt vicious, maddened by this great ape standing there. He'd gone too far. I fired past his head just to show him I meant business.

'There's more left. Come on, get overboard. Wait a minute — chuck us that dough you've got first.'

Tookley didn't move. He stood there like the trunk of a tree.

'Frisk him, Duggie. Get that money. I'll keep you covered.'

Tookley moved to the side of the truck. Then Duggie lurched against me, jolting his fist on my arm, so that the gun fell: and stumbled against me, and there was a snap — I heard the snap — and when I tried to pull my wrists apart they were locked in the cuffs.

'Sit down there on your swag,' Duggie said, panting. 'You won't hurt anything. I've got the stuff we want out of it.'

Tookley picked up the automatic carefully and wrapped it in a handkerchief; and when he spoke it was in a quiet, tired voice: 'In case you don't know it, you're under arrest for murder,' he said.

THE OLD MAN WAS AN EMPEROR

I went up on that evening in October to see Danny Calhoun. He had his cap pulled down, his shirt sleeves rolled up, and he was drinking. He told me this:

They put him away today, out in that old cemetery where they've put some of the best of this country. It doesn't matter about the brambles there, the green damp, and the tilted headstones. It's the ground that counts. I got a crazy idea that's Australia, and you can't take it away from them. Never mind about the time of its drift, the span of its loneliness; the bones of its dark hunters and the beasts that roared in its nights: that moved unwilled with the current of its coal and its chalk and its gems and lighted the air out over its swamps.

It belonged to no one then. But it's ours now. Our dead have flagged it; the good hearts and the good minds have sanctified and consecrated it.

And my old man is among that lot.

He was nothing, but he was an emperor. He was a judge and jury. He was a ring of councillors, and the wise man at their head. His kingdom was a house of weatherboard, his throne that rickety old chair in the kitchen, and his subjects were six kids and a woman. His authority was just.

The sceptre of his life and the standard of his leadership were his hands.

I know all about those hands. They were brown like the skin of the potato, mapped with seams on the back and knuckled like marbles; the hair on the fingers was bushed and golden; the palm was grooved like water streaks in clay; the flesh was hard and shiny as worn sandpaper. They were big hands and thick hands, misshapen and cicatrized.

I'm glad I got a photograph of his hands. One worth framing. It's going to stay on the mantelshelf as long as I'm alive; my kids will take care of it then. I took it myself with a box Brownie, a cheap, crank old thing that I won in a foot race at the school sports on St. Patrick's Day, but it took pictures all right.

The old boy laughed when I got him to pose his hands. He hadn't thought about them the way I had. He said it was silly. But there was some sort of pride in his voice. He knew I was right.

I'm glad he saw that picture. It looked good, enlarged. He was pleased.

Think of those hands.

He won a fight with them; he won Mum with them. They used to be funny telling the story. They'd laugh soft and loud by turns, taunt each other, and blush and look modest now and then.

I thought he was the biggest swell ever set foot in Bundaberg — that was Mum. I blessed myself three times when I saw him; once for fear that he was going to make up to me and twice for fear that he wasn't.

Scrubbing the stairs, she was, when I hit the door, with her bottom towards me. The view was lovely. Straightaway, I made up my mind to stay in that hotel and no other.

You looked so handsome; so tall and elegant in your cutaway coat and your herringbone vest. It was cream, I remember, with little cornelians for buttons. But that hat!

What was wrong with the hat? It had the curliest brim you ever saw on a beaver.

It never suited you. Made your head look funny.

Funny! It's the mo you should have been taking exception to! Seeing pictures of myself now, I wonder what in God's truth ever made me paste the tail of a horse on my top lip.

It was a beautiful mo, and don't say anything against it.

I used to step in then and tell them I didn't want to hear about each other's good and bad in the way of dress and manners. I wanted to hear about the fight.

The old man told me: Norah was shook on a big cane-cutter with more hair on his chest than a goat and more cotton in his head than a Belfast mill. His name was Johnny McDougall.

I wasn't shook on him, said Mum. He was shook on me.

Now, you did like him you'll not be denying it. Until I came along. I'd just made a big clean-up shearing on the Downs; so I had money to show her the good things of the town. When it petered out I was going to cut cane.

You didn't look the part of a cane-cutter.

I didn't look the part of a monkey, either, but I could scratch with the best of 'em! Well, to get on with it, this McDougall didn't like me going around with his girl. He warned me twice, I remember. Told me he'd pull the face off me and hang it on the back of my head.

You, he said to me the second time. I'll have you get it into your thick skull that the girl, Norah Shean, who works at the Port Hotel, belongs to me, and if you don't stop making up to her, God help you if I lift me fists.

I passed him off with a grin. I didn't want to fight the sod. Not without stilts and a bit of padding on me, anyway. He had the reputation of being the best grass-fighter round there. Fight like a threshing machine, everybody said. He had the fear in them all. I felt that fear, too, in a way I didn't like.

Yes, said Mum; and everybody knew you felt it. They spread it all over town.

So, no wonder it got to your little pink shells. Me, taking cheek from this big standover merchant and running away. I suppose after the second time the whole town thought I'd cram my tail between my legs and scoot like the Pooka himself was after me.

Well, they were right.

But they weren't really right, said Mum.

Yes, they were, Dad said. It was in my heart to leave, for I'm not one for trouble, though I can handle myself in it. What I was going to do was get you to come with me. Your mother, Danny. But she wouldn't budge.

There I was asking her, and she as cold as charity. Indignant and disappointed-looking, saying all sorts of things but none of them near the point. Finally she out with it why she wouldn't come with me.

She said quietly: I don't think I could be happy with a weakling. If a man shows he's a coward in one way he'll show it in another, and life is full of bullies of one sort or the other.

I said with my lip stuck out: You think I'm not game to fight that big mug for you?

It's not for me, she said. It's for your self-respect.

I was as mad as a woodheap. I knew I was mad. There was a looking-glass in the room, and I kept looking at my white face in it, and my flashing eyes, and feeling glad I was mad. Making a play for myself, admiring my fury and invigorated by it.

I said: I'll belt the ears off him. I'll use his guts for neckties. I'll smash him to a pulp. I'll do this and I'll do that, I told her. But I had a hunch I wouldn't. I knew it was just bravado in the seconds that I thought about it. But I think she believed me.

I did, Mum said.

Sure, she believed me, for the next tick she ran up, put her arms around me, and said: No, don't! Don't fight him. He'll kill you. He's too big and strong for you. Let him go; I don't care if you never fight him. I'll go with you. We'll clear out and he'll trouble us no more.

Well that's what did it. I remember I stood there, calm,

feeling her warm body against mine, listening to her crying softly, and I knew how much she thought of me. I knew, too, how much I thought of her. But I felt humiliated. She could have barged me all night telling me I was a cur and a coward, and I might have taken that. But when she started to coddle me and protect me with that anxious sincerity the rage come up in me: and if I'd been the midget of the world I'd have been a giant then, with more spoil in me for McDougall than for a dozen Orangemen that spat in the eye of the Pope.

Too big for me, is he? I said. Kill me, will he? We'll see about that.

And I slammed that door and went looking for the man; but I didn't find him that night. I found him next day, and I was the same man, only worse if anything. It was Saturday, and the cutters were in the pub bar, and him among them, this McDougall.

No, said Mum, don't tell it. It's too awful.

I called his name, said Dad, and I pulled him around by the shoulder and said to him: You mug, I'll wipe the floor with you! He stood gaping for a second; then he roared laughing. He couldn't have done a worse thing. I didn't know whether I could lick him, but I was determined to die doing it. And that laugh of his only set my determination all the more.

Listen, I said: I'm telling you to get it into your ugly nut that Norah Shean is my girl. My girl, see! And if you've got anything to say against that, come out the back.

He came all right, and they made a circle for us in the pub yard. I stripped to the waist, but he only chucked off his coat. He had a grin all over his face. He sparred on his own for a minute. Then he charged. He nearly took my head off with his first punch. I fell groggy in the dust, and I heard your mother crying out: Stop it! Stop it! But my old girl never reared a jib. I got up, and I spit on my fists, and got into him. I heard him grunt when I landed one in his guts and it gave me heart.

I learned two things quick: I learned he depended on his punch, and I learned he was slow moving. His weight held him back. I used my advantages. I scuttled in, chopped his face, and ducked out again. I took his fists on my arms till the skin was peeled and the muscles went dead. But I hung on. My fettle was good, and the kick soon come back into my arms. I had a funny sense that my fists were weighted, and I threw them like ramrods.

I didn't hear a sound from the crowd. It was queer. The dust was like a cattleyard, stinging the eyes and drying the tongue.

Then I got him a beauty. I ducked a left and drove my right into his belly. It gave like a cushion. I brought the right up under his chin. He fell back, and I over with the left, hooking it down on the edge of his jaw.

He fell. He got up groggy. I spit on my fists again and whaled in. He was tough. He knocked me about that time, but I put three under his heart, and he bit the dust again. I was fighting mad, I can tell you. I pulled him by the shirt and he staggered up. He was like a blind man. His punches were weaker. I took some of them to give him worse.

Then he crashed one on my chin that I thought had done for me. Noises in the brain and a flapping darkness as I fell; a new taste in my mouth and my tongue soaking in it.

But I got up. I saw him blundering towards me. I whirled aside and behind him, the fog getting out of my brain. He come again, fetching his left in a straightening arc. I backstepped a bit, and that pelted him right in to meet my left. The jolt sent a shiver of pain up my arm, but it stopped him dead. I saw his eyes roll, and his arms fell at his sides.

They were cheering then, yelling like maniacs, telling me to finish him off.

I slugged and slammed him. Jaw, body. Jaw, body. He was like a slowly falling tree. Then he was at my feet, still. The dust was thick; there was a drip-drip over my eyes. I backed away spitting out blood and dust, and grimacing my sore face to see if it worked.

They were slapping me on the back, telling me we'd been fighting for an hour, saying they hadn't seen a fight like that in

71

years; and all the rest of it. But I was looking for Norah, your mother. Do you know where she was?

There in the clearing dust was McDougall, a mask of dirt on his face and a thick scum of it on his bloody lips; his left eye up like a painted bubble, and blood spilling out of his split eyebrow; there, snorting as he breathed, in a way that frightened me, with the blood bubbling at his nostrils. But over him, on her knees, was Norah, crying as she cleaned his face, crying in a sort of joy and sorrow mixed, muttering the poor man, the poor man, and abusing me something woeful, telling me I was a brute and a fiend, the cruellest coot she ever laid eyes on, and she didn't want to know me.

Women! The longer I live the less I know about them.

That's how Dad told it to me. He won Mum, and he did it with his hands.

I came first, and was three when Mikey came, and six when Mum had the twins.

I thought a lot of those hands even then. He'd get me in those hands and throw me up and swing me on to his back. He was the strongest man in the world, and I was a kid on Goliath, looking down on the distant footpath and bumping my head on the stars. Funny, when you think how, at the end, I could lift him from his sick bed on to the veranda. I lifted him, and he was light, as light as I must have been.

With those hands he built his house. Only a hut it was, but it kept us warm. And the rain and the wind passed it by. He cut the timber for it, and put it up on good high ground in that northern country where he was ring-barking. I used to go out with him sometimes in the morning. He'd pick up the other workers at their camp, and go into the scrub; I watched him cut a clean circle out of the tree trunks, driving his blade into sap that leaked out like gum, with a smell that was strongest on the night wind; and I looked at the clean red and yellow chips on the ground and I felt sad for the tree, knowing it was going to die. I was a funny kid, I suppose.

The hut outlasted the job by years: It's still standing there, I'd say, for that's how he built it.

Yes, he had good hands.

He drove us around the bush with them, in an old jalopy that he got for a song from a shearer called Tommy the Pea who went broke one summer in Tumbarumba. And he showed us kids how to fight with them. And he taught us how to work. He husked corn with them, dug spuds, pulled peas, shore sheep and tamed horses.

He pitched the tent by the side of the old bus at the shearing, and that way he made more money; and he had us with him all the time and we had him.

I helped him pick up the spuds as they lay in their row, and helped him bag them. But I wasn't worth the five bob a week he paid me. When the sleet came he worked with a bag over his head; and on the frozen mornings of frost and snow he kept a fire bucket in the field to warm his hands now and then.

He never worried when the kids kept coming. His hands could do better. They had to do better. He worked harder. He took a pencil and ran our budget. He kept our bellies full; saw we got enough.

He saved Mum's life with his hands: I'd say he did. In the floodtime it was, back of Barcaldine; the rain had come over nights and days till there was no other sound but rain, and you could forget there was ever any other sound. It came in over the floor and we paddled in it; it stacked drift against the door alive with snakes and lizards.

The house was a boat that never moved, and there was no way of leaving the boat. But the waters were going when it happened; the rain had stopped, the sky was the colour of putty, and we were in the middle of a seeping lagoon as far as you could see, reflecting the straggling shadows of depressed trees.

He yelled at me in the evening: Danny!

What's up?

Your mother, he said. She's sick. Get the kids and keep them in the back room.

I was bewildered by the look on his face and frightened in my bewilderment. I ran into the bedroom without listening to any more. He followed me. Mum was lying on the bed, groaning. Her face was sweating. Her eyelids were black; when she drew them back there was an ache in her eyes.

She just smiled at me, and took my hand in hers that was so burning, but I could say nothing.

He said: Danny, listen to me. Your mother's been taken sick; sudden.

Tell him, Mum said.

Danny, he said, you're big now. You've got sense. Your mother's going to have a baby. But there's no doctor. She's in pain; it might hurt. She might scream. You understand?

I was just nodding at him, hardly understanding.

He said: that's why I want you to take the kids into the back room. Amuse them there. Do anything, but keep them there; look after them and tell them everything's all right.

He pushed me out with a pat on the back, and I knew by that pat he was depending on me. I felt glad to be depended on.

I got Mikey and the other two, young Tommy with his silky shiny head like an acorn, and Bobby, his twin, and I took them into the back room, lit the kerosene lamp, and started reading and explaining the comics to them.

When she wailed they looked at me in puzzlement; then, when she screamed, in fear. They cluttered up close to me. Mikey went to the door.

No, I said, don't go out there. Don't you want me to read you some more?

What's up with Mummy? he said.

Nothing. Come on, sit down here with me.

She screamed again, not much, but high. I tried to raise my voice over the top of it. I went on. But they weren't listening to me. All their eyes were fixed on the door — their eyes in their still heads.

Mikey began to cry: I want to see Mummy, he sobbed.

You can't, I told him. Stop crying.

No, I want to see her.

Stop it, I roared in a low voice. Stop it!

His crying made the others start, one after the other. I tried to hush them. I coaxed and threatened them. They got on my nerves. The screams terrified me. I wanted to cry, too — I wanted to rush out beyond that door and see what was happening to her, see if I could do anything. But I had to stay there, in that room lit yellow and filled with shadows in the corners; blinded to something my ears reported to me and tortured me to witness.

Then all at once they stopped crying, them with me, and we all looked into each other's faces; and I suppose the look of wide-eyed curiosity and wonder on theirs was the image on mine.

A baby was crying out there — a snuffling, wide-mouthed bawling. They whispered to me. We waited. The crying stopped. Then the door-knob turned, and he came in tired and strained in look, but with a light on his face and shine in his eyes.

He said, smiling: You'll have to remember yourselves, now, gentlemen, for you've got a sister.

No! No! Not yet; you can see her after a while, when your mother's had sleep.

Good boy, Danny, he said to me. Come on, we'll go out and get some tea.

When the ground was passable the doctor came, and he said he couldn't have done better himself. Dad wasn't there when he said that. He was out on the job again, hunting dingoes, setting the traps, laying the baits, watching the waterholes, his hands on his gun.

We came to the city, and he worked there; he needed a steady job that brought in a regular cheque, he said, and we needed a chance to get some schooling.

He worked hard with his hands, and we got it.

There was no chance of his winning a lottery to pay the expense when Mikey got sick. He had to rely on those hands.

He took Mikey to the best doctor, and he told the doctor he'd pay him as much as he could and work the rest out. He'd cut his hedge, mow his lawn, clean his car — do anything until the bill was paid.

He went on doing it after Mikey died, for that was his principle; even thought the doc wanted to call it quits, he went on doing it. He owed no man anything, he was proud to tell us.

And all through his time he cut and gouged and knocked his hands; the callouses rose like horn on them. He poisoned them and they puffed, and turned red and purple; but he had good blood, and the germs built their fortresses and their citadel and killed their enemies; and they were restored.

And that buttressed our security again.

You think a man's crazy, maybe.

But his hands were his ensign, and ours.

They make a man in bronze; he sailed the seas, so they put a telescope in his hands; they raise a statue of an explorer, and they give him a flyveil and a billycan; a million men die as one and they build a cenotaph. There were no speeches for my old man; no marches; no draped coffins; no flags at half mast.

But he did a job as well as any.

He was a worker.

And I took his hands, the symbol of his greatness, to reverence and to cherish.

And I'm glad I did.

HELP

A blocky man stood on the kerb looking across the street. These were the facets of the scene: pigeons strutting and preening; rumbling trucks and dinning cars; men smoking, yarning, leering, leaning outside the relief quarters — spitting and yarning men; frowsy men; men that were not men at all, but loafing parasites, whose kids had spindly legs and hollow eyes, and who let their wives drudge themselves grey and asthmatic in factories; stray dogs, a church, and a newsboy.

The man on the corner stood facing these things, and he thought.

He felt his stubbled cheek go cool as a shadow slanted across it. A hand touched him lightly.

'Bud?'

'Yeah?' he answered.

'Sorry to trouble you. Hot, ain't it? Mind if I bum a smoke?'

'Only got the makin's. Roll you one. Hot, all right.'

'Thanks, pal.'

'Nice day?'

'Yeah . . . Nice in the country now, eh? Smell o'summer — nice. Scent's not so good here.' He laughed, coarse and hearty. His hairy-fingered, strong hand took the cigarette.

'Got a match? Sorry to trouble you . . .'

''S' all right. No trouble.'

Matches rattled. One flared. The man on the kerb took them back with his short, stubby fingers.

'A smoke's good.'

'Glad to oblige. Say, anything wrong?'

'Just a bit hot, pal. Smelly. Gritty. Noisy. I like the country.'

He drew on the cigarette.

'I hate to trouble you . . .'

'What's up? Broke?'

'No, no nothin' like that. Nothin' like that. But — I was wantin' to go to the church . . .'

'Yeah.'

'Where is it, do y' know?'

'Sure — just over there . . .'

'Say, feller, I'm sorry to trouble you . . .' He held the cigarette at his side. 'But I'm wantin' to go there . . .'

'Yeah.'

'Well . . . well . . . my lights . . .'

The man on the kerb was silent.

The other went on with quickened speech: 'I know I'm a goddam encumbrance. I'm ashamed . . . I hate troublin' people. I . . .'

'Sorry, I didn't notice.'

'Come all of a sudden . . . Only been home three months. Only been here, in the city, a week. The quacks couldn't do anything . . .'

'How'd it happen?'

'Nothin' much. Ground just blew up in front of us. Just a blue, blindin' flash. Fixed my nerves. Just come against me now . . . A strong, blue flash . . .'

'Yeah, I know. I was in the last one. Argonne.'

'God, were you! You know, then . . .'

'Might clear up.'

'Might. Got faith, anyway. They say faith helps . . . works wonders. But, hell — I'm bitter about it, and I won't say I ain't. There's beautiful things to see. I wish it was a leg, or an arm . . .'

'Faith's the only thing,' said the man on the kerb, reflecting.

'They say a man gets used to being blind.' The other drew hard on his cigarette, and the smoke trickled out of his mouth. 'They say some fellers can get about better than those with sight. You get a sort of mental eye . . . another sense to make up for it . . . Yeah, I was wantin' to go to the church. Will you see me there . . . ?'

'Put your arm through mine.'

'Thanks, pal. It's swell of you. Sorry to trouble you . . .'

''S nothin'.'

The scene was apparently unchanged. The pigeons preened and strutted. The street was busy and noisy. Dogs strayed. The church stood calm. Outside the relief quarters, the men were as before. Only the newsboy changed. He addressed nobody in particular:

'Hey, there's a funny thing.'

Men turned their heads, stared.

'What?'

'That feller — not the one with the cigarette. The one that was standin' on the kerb. See him helpin' the other guy across the road?'

Three said in turn:

'Well?'

'Yeah?'

'What's funny about it?'

The kid said: 'He's blind himself.'

AFTER THE CUT OUT

*H*e felt the first gnaw of fear about five. He had been drinking all the afternoon, shouting for all comers, drifting into their conversation, leaving them, drifting around the bar. Fat faces and thin, brown and blue eyes, teeth, lips, laughs in the throat and laughs from the belly, coming and going and gone.

Now the birl of sound was high. The pub was crowded. He wanted it to stay that way until the coming of the light, protection against the dark he saw deepening against the outside windows and through the door. He butted into a group and laid a note on the counter and cried genially to the barman to fill 'em up for the boys. He wanted their friendship, their comradeliness, their hospitality.

But the time was beating him and winning the battle. He heard the sound die down and as it did he swallowed with fear. He looked at the dwindling mob and his eyes were startled with something of terror. Hastily he barged about, seeking their companionship, inviting their fellowship, trying to perpetuate the social atmosphere and embracing it against his dread.

Then there was no sound. He was lolling over the bar. He felt the tap on his shoulder: 'Come on, mate, fair go. We're closing now.'

He looked up like a fugitive, at the empty saloon, the battered face of the barman clutching a broom.

'What about you and me having a drink?' he cried.

'No thanks,' the barman said shortly. 'Be a sport, come on.'

The barman took his arm and he let himself be guided out through the door. The light inside vanished with the slam of the door, the grate of the key in the lock. There were still little groups about. He stumbled into them, slapping men on the back, saying desperately: 'How's she going, mate?' And: 'What's the time, cobber?' Or: 'Feel like a drink, just you and me?' They passed him off, and left him and then he was alone on the deserted pub corner, and the fear was solid in him and he felt stricken.

This was it. This was what he feared. Every one of them was the same, every country town. On the stroke of nightfall they became shells. Long, empty streets lined with still lights, lighting nothing except the shadowy, empty roadway and the few cars hulked against the kerbs. The shops were blind. Everybody had gone. Life had folded up. A great horror had driven the townspeople away, and in a while the grass would grow in the streets, the rust eat away the cars, and the lights burn on through the deserted day into the deserted night until they burned out: and gradually the blackness would creep over and engulf the town until it was a black ghost with no beacon to mark its whereabouts.

He looked about him with nervous apprehension and started off down the street. He heard his footfalls and they were like a drum calling attention to his presence. They kept the same tempo and the same loudness. Then the tempo changed and the loudness increased. He wondered why. Then it occurred to him that the extra loudness was not coming from his own footfalls. He stopped and looked quickly behind

81

him. The deserted street stretched in dismal perspective. He walked again and looked swiftly, unexpectedly, around. There was no one in sight.

At the first side street he halted. He stood on the kerb. He looked down one way and saw the wall of darkness and the lights ballooning away in the distance. He heard footsteps, and his blood galloped. He turned casually around and peered down the street. Then to his right, in the darkness of a door-front, he saw the red point of a cigarette.

He walked across the street. He went along by the lifeless windows and glancing back saw a figure in an overcoat and smoking a cigarette behind him. He slowed his pace. He felt the pace of the man behind him slow down. He stopped to look in the lighted window of a stationer's shop. He saw nothing there. Though he was ostensibly looking at the cards and pencils, calendars, books and figurines, his eyes were swivelled. They saw the overcoated man stop and look in the window.

He walked on, more quickly, and when he came to the Greek's he was breathing heavily. He sat down and ordered. The restaurant was empty. A plasticine Greek stood silently behind the counter with his arms folded. A mantel radio on a shelf was playing a Scottish medley. He waited in a sweat of fear, his back to the street.

The overcoated man came in and sat down at one of the tables opposite the cubicle he was in. The man took off his hat, put it under the chair. He put his elbows on the marble table-top, clasped his hands and rested his chin on them. The man in the cubicle tried to place him. He saw mouths and eyes and teeth. He thought he had seen him before in the pub. He remembered the hair but the nose was somebody else's. He knew the chin, but he couldn't remember the overcoat.

He jumped up and strode across to the table: 'You, what's your caper?'

The man looked up startled: 'Caper?'

'What are you following me for?'

The surprise turned to bewilderment: 'Following you? What's the matter with you, old chap? I'm not following you.'

'Keep away from me, that's all.' He said it savagely, fearfully, and turned quickly and went out into the night. He looked through the window. The startled puzzlement was still on the man's face. It relieved him.

He looked about him and went back down the street. He stopped in the darkness of an awning. He saw two men on the opposite side. Slowly they walked across. One of them was big, with a grubby white shirt open at the neck and swollen by his belly, the other was weedy, thin-faced and dressed in a sports suit.

He kept walking, but one of them called him: 'Hey, mate.'

He stopped, trembling, his fists clenched, sweat prickling his body. They came up to him.

'Got a match on you, pal?' the big man said.

'No, go to hell!'

He backed and broke into a run. The wind cut like a knife of ice against his face. It stung his eyes. He legs ached. His chest throbbed with pain. He had to slow up. He fell down in the long grass on the footpath. He heard them running, the light and the heavy. He put his arms about his head to cushion the kicks. Their feet galloped in a tattoo like kettledrums right up in mounting loudness to the threshold of his ears and he shut his eyes tight and screwed up his face. But there was no sound. There were no blows.

In consternation he looked up and about him. He was under the circle of radiance from the lone street light. He looked down the empty street. He heard shunting in the distance. There was nothing else.

Sobbing with exertion, he went down a lonely way, past a few silent houses with a light here and there in their windows. None of them belonged to him. They were all part of the town that had closed its doors to him and cast him off. He came back into the main street. He felt a wind rising, and it went with the emptiness and the eeriness.

He walked down towards the bottom end, and his footfalls unnerved him. They threw out echoes, betraying him. He sat down and took off his boots and carried them under his arms. He made no sound now. But the footfalls continued. He heard them. When he stopped, they stopped. When he started, they started. He looked ahead and behind him, and behind him he saw a figure step back into a dark door-front. He stared till his eyes watered. He saw it move again, just the vague drawing of darkness from darkness and the melting back again.

He walked quickly to the corner and turned it. He stopped. Cautiously, he peered around, but he couldn't see anything distinguishable, only movement in the patches of darkness.

'Hey, you!'

The sound jerked him around, and he saw idling towards him from the side street the weedy man and the big one.

'What's the big idea of — '

He didn't hear the rest. He ran straight down the main street, and he didn't stop till he reached the police station. The one word: *Police* stopped him. He waited till his shuddering breath came back. He stared back the way he had come. There was no sign of the big man and the weedy one, but there was the presence he felt was following him before he came on them again the second time.

It was blanketing itself in the darkness by the buildings, melting into the shop fronts and materialising. He half ran up the steps into the police station.

He burst out: 'Get them. They're after me. They're following me.'

The sergeant stared at him, the boots under his arm, his tortured face; and the young constable sitting back on the tilted chair put his newspaper down.

'Who's after you?'

'Out there. I dunno.'

'What have you done?'

'I've done nothing.'

'Talk sense, man. If somebody's after you they must be after you for something.'

'I've got a roll on me. That's what they're after. They want to do me in. You got to lock me up. You got to let me stay here.'

He saw the young constable look at the sergeant and he saw the return of that meaning look. The constable went outside into the street. He came back shaking his head.

'I tell you I saw them. I tell you — '

'Who are you?' snapped the sergeant over the words. 'What do you do? Where'd you come from?'

'I'm a shearer. I come in today from Moombala. We cut out there first run this morning.'

'Where are you going?'

'I got a pen at Glenman, and I'm off out there tomorrow. Look, you got to keep me here till then. Till the morning.'

'We can't keep you here. We'll be knocking off in a few minutes. Why don't you go to a hotel?'

'No! Worse, that is. I don't sleep, see.'

'You can leave your money here if you like.'

'I don't leave it anywhere. It's on me and it stays on me.' He trusted nobody.

'All right. I suggest you go to a hotel then. Tom, go out there with him and take him along to Savage's.'

He dragged on his boots, left them unlaced. He went along the way he had come with the young policeman who disdainfully said nothing. Every dark door-front he peered into held eyes watching him. They stopped in front of a hotel.

'Okay,' the policeman said, 'you'll be set now. Ring the bell and go in and get yourself a good night's sleep. Don't hit it so hard next time.'

He watched the policeman walk down the street and he wet his lips and tried to make up his mind whether or not to push the bell. He saw something move again in a patch of darkness and strained his eyes to identify it. But he couldn't. He turned suddenly and walked swiftly. His footfalls rang out. He half-ran. The clatter of his feet reverberated in the emptiness. He broke into a full run. He passed a lighted door, stopped and ran back and hurried inside.

It was a hall, packed with women of all ages seated on

forms. There was a woman on the platform speaking . . .' If women are to maintain the rights that have been won for them, if they are to uphold the social and moral sanctities and ensure that their children are . . .'

The words went into sound, all sound, pausy and highpitched, and he kept turning his head towards the door expectantly. He saw several women looking at him curiously. He didn't know what kind of club it was. He wasn't interested. He was glad of the light, the body of people. They gave him security. Then he heard clapping, and the women were standing up, and he realised the meeting was over. They began to disperse towards the door.

He stood in the entrance, watching them drift away, watching the hall empty. Desperately he stopped a young woman: 'Pardon me, lady, do you mind if I walk along with you?'

She looked alarmed, muttered something low in her throat and hurried away.

An elderly woman put her hand on his sleeve: 'Excuse me, are you ill?'

He grabbed at the concern on her face: 'Yes, I don't feel well. Not well at all. But I'll be all right when I get walking. Can I walk along with you?'

'Certainly.'

He stepped along beside her. He told her briefly he was a stranger; knew no one. He said he was broke. He thought hopefully that she might ask him into her place and they'd talk and maybe have a drink. Then he was silent.

They walked along in silence. He heard her footfalls, short, quick, beating between his own. His own trod on the top of hers. Hers were silent, then rushed in on his again. He looked straight ahead. He was just moving, the pavement clattering and thumping under him. He saw movement in the black wells of doorways, creeping elusively in the shadows, here, there, all about and about.

Then, suddenly, he was aware that the footfalls were not the same. His were, but the others had changed. They were not short and quick any longer. They were longer, softer, more measured. He knew them. He looked quickly to the person beside him. The woman was gone. In her place was the man in the overcoat. The man who had looked in the stationer's window, who had sat down in the restaurant, who had walked along behind him.

With a cry he pelted away, running madly. He stopped for an instant and looked back, and, fifty yards away, standing in the emptiness, was the woman in a pose of incredulity and amazement. Then he kept on running. He didn't know where. He kept going. His legs ached and the sap of power drained off leaving them rubber. His lungs sucked at whistling air. His chest was crushed and heaving with pain.

He stumbled and staggered. Then he stopped dead. His teeth chattered. The moon was thundering towards him. There was a hammering and a roaring in his ears. He stared, terrified. He shrieked in the hideous glare of the orb and fell senseless.

In the morning he found himself, damp and stiff, in the long grass by the railway line. He saw the station half a mile away. He heard the clop of hooves. He saw a yardman hosing the footpath in front of a hotel across the street. The sun crept warmly over the buildings of the waking town, and the shadows were all soft and warm. He checked his wallet.

Thank God that's over, he told himself. Next time I'll go home for sure between sheds, or go to the shed and stay there. No more of this coming into bloody bush towns with a roll for me.

He had said it before. He'd say it again.

And that's how Little George Orris, the gun shearer, came to be known in the outback as a bit of a hatter. Not that he cared.

TALE OF A DEAD MAN

*H*e staggered up the stairs, turned the doorknob, lay down on the bed and died. His spirit rose, walked down the stairs and out into the street. The street was a hard black road of light. There was no one about. He went down the street, and stood under a bleak lamp in a cage above him. There was a thick smear of blood from his head on the tall pole. A wind thrummed in the telegraph wires: a chill singing.

He went south, and entered the black furrow of a lane. At a spot in the deeper darkness he stopped. He had been there before. The snaggled fences leaned towards him from either side. A cat sprang with a metallic clatter from a garbage can and curdled on a post into a black bulk dotted twice with green. Suddenly its back arched, and the hair along the arch was like a fin of raised prickles. It stared with a stony caution. He went towards it, and the cat spat in terror and was gone.

His blood, or some of it, was there at his feet. He saw himself lying there, and a hand was jerking the knife out of his back. He was on one side of his face and it was cold against the gravel. He was being roughed. Hands tore through his pockets.

'That's about it.'

'Come on, then; let's get out of this.'

He went down the lane, away from his dying self that stumbled in agony to its feet, and he met himself coming into the lane, and there were two men with him. And he was happy with a few drinks in him, and he was saying: 'We're all good pals together, ain't we?'

And they were saying: 'Sure we are. Sure we are.'

There was one on each side of him, and they were holding his arms in the loose friendly way of revellers. And one of them said: 'You got a lotta money there, Tommy. Too much money for one feller. You let us look after it for you, eh?'

And he said: 'We're all good pals together, ain't we?'

And the other said, playing the same tune as his mate: 'We'll look after it for you, Tommy boy. You pass it over to Fred and me.'

But he just went on singing and feeling glad he was alive, and making hell because the eyes of the world were on him. He was drunk, but he wasn't so drunk that he didn't know it wasn't his own hand around his breast pocket. He said: 'What are you doing, Fred? Mitts off.'

And Fred said: 'How d'ye like that? How d'ye like that?'

And they went on down the lane, and they weren't singing any more. He was singing, but they weren't. They were silent as if they'd stepped out of character. And suddenly they stopped him short; and the thin man rapped out viciously: 'Hand over that dough, you, quick!' And the other snapped, with a grip on his shoulder: 'Come on, mug. We've got no time for games.'

And that was it. The sudden bewilderment, the shock of realisation, the fearful protests, the struggle — his head smashed back against the fence, the raw fists jolting his brain into a smudge of light, the knife in his back. That was it.

He went on alone now out of the lane and into a cold street, a street of tall goblin houses smelling of gas and long-nosed landlords; a narrow chimney where the air was ice and the currents capered with tatters of paper in the gutters, and some old man coughed on a balcony. Along the street, and into another, and on to the corner pub. There he stood, under the shadowy awning, peering through the mosaic walls into the emptiness of the bar, different from what it was a few hours ago.

A few hours ago when he was in there, chiacking the chinny barmaid with the wrinkles in her rouge and the magpie personality; caught up in the social atmosphere, watching the potbellied publican pulling on the shiny taps, listening to the sustained bagpipe drone of conversation. But lonely, because he was solitary; solitary because he knew nobody.

And then all at once they were there — the lean, hungry-looking one, and the one with the stubble and the eyes that shone like syrup; and talking; and the money coming out and the drinks coming up; the laughing and the joking; the one about the old woman on the train, and the old boy crying in the bath room. It was good, and hell, they were funny.

And they stayed together singing, and when they left they were singing; and that's how it was when they dawdled on, three of a kind, towards the lane.

And now it was silent there under the pub verandah, and he was silent with it. And he felt only the jar of his lacerated nerves torn and left like quivering strands in his body. He felt the noise of shock in his spirit. And his spirit was weeping with rage and hate because it had been cheated.

You'll know it all back there; tomorrow you'll know it. There'll be you, old Jamieson, the stationmaster; with the grubby uniform of trousers and vest, and the cap pushed back on your grey hair. You'll be saying: 'But, good God, it can't be true. Only the other day I shook hands with him. I shook hands with him only the other day. And he waved to me from the train window.'

He waved to everybody. He waved to his mother, and his father, and his kid sister.

He waved to them that were jealous of his going to the city; getting away from the sleepy town: those glued in their grooves angry with themselves because they hadn't the courage to leave and make a go of it in the big town. And they, when they heard of it, wouldn't feel so bad.

He was enraged for those who would sorrow for his death. He went back the way he had come, through the lane again, hunting the vultures, and it was strange — because he knew where they were. They were in the top room of a house a block away from the lane, and two blocks from where he had a lodging.

As soon as he was in the room with them, as they sat at a table under a naked fly-specked bulb, he knew that there was a controlled menace between them. There was brooding antagonism and it was building. The lean, hungry-looking man said: 'He asked for it, and he got it.'

And the other said: 'But you didn't have to kill him.'

'Me? Listen, you're in it as much as I am. You killed him as much as I did.'

'All right. Keep your hair on.'

'You got it straight — if the coppers question us, we don't know a thing.'

'I'm not frightened of coppers.'

'Keep your block, that's all.'

The short man with the syrupy eyes got up, and he said fiercely: 'Never mind telling me to keep my block. You watch your own step. That's all you've got to do.'

And the lean man said: 'Don't shout. Every bastard in the place'll hear you.'

The short man glared, panting: 'I'm damned if I'll be in on that murder rap! It was you that stuck the knife in him. You didn't have to. We had him all right.'

The lean man stood up, his thin face drawn like a wedge: 'Listen, you know something. You've got cold feet all ready. Whingeing like a dingo. Well, get this. If you blab a word, if you put me in to save your own measly skin, you'll come a gutser. Because I'll tell 'em you did it. I'll drag you in as deep as you drag me. Understand?'

The short man screwed up his face in a sour fear and hate. He said: 'What'd you do with the knife?'

'I chucked it in a drain. You seen me.'

'No, I didn't. You were mad to do that. Say they find that knife?'

'They won't find it unless they scour the ocean.'

'I dunno,' said the short man. 'You should have kept it, and we could have broken it up.'

'Ah, shut up, willya? You've got your tenner, and he's dead; so shut up.'

The short man scrabbled in his clothing. His eyes were bulging, hard and strained. He lit a cigarette. He spun the match into a corner, and drummed his fingers on the table: 'I thought he had more than twenty in that roll.'

The lean man looked sharply at him: 'You saying I got more than you did?'

'No, I'm not saying that.'

'Well, I didn't. You seen me count to — ten for you, ten for me. You think I maybe kept back an extra tenner, do yer?'

'And, listen,' said the short man suddenly; 'what about the people that seen us with him? There's always people; bloody people. Say they seen you if they never seen you. What about that barmaid?'

'What about her?'

'She knows we drank with him.'

'She wasn't taking that much notice.'

'What? That piece?' The short man said. 'Eyes like a hawk, her. She seen us all right, and she'll be the first to say her bit when they find that bushwhacker.'

'You're shouting again.'

'What if I am? What if I am shouting? If you can't see what we're up against, I can. We're mugs. You bungled the job. It's your fault.'

'Sit down and shut your mouth!'

'You stuck the knife in him, you didn't have to. And Christ, I'm not taking any rap for murder. I'm not doing life for you or anyone else.'

He was white and sweating: 'I'm out of this. You hear? I'm out of it. I — '

'Shut up!'

And the lean man struck, and they fought. They rolled on the floor like tigers. The table overturned. Chairs skated against the wall. They grunted. And the short man, with eyes like marbles, choked and squalled from the hands at this throat. In desperate panic, he punched a gash over the other's eye, lashed with his legs, and flung him off like a dog.

He ran down the stairs, and the spirit of the murdered man went after him, and with him to the stone building with the white light, and inside, and heard him babble, and saw the police activity, and the confession papers.

And then he left.

He wandered back to the shabby room. He looked at the startling red counterpane and the dead eyes that stared back; looked at his clay on the bed . . . and waited.

THE WEB

*T*he old man was still strange in the house, but he had encompassed the family, his daughter, her husband, both, except the boy. The boy seemed to be walking around the outskirts of his friendliness, now and then edging over the line, but scuttling back again. He sensed about him a manner he could not fathom.

Now the boy threw his schoolbag down, and took an apple from the sideboard. Slowly, he tiptoed towards his grandfather and cautiously moved all round him, taking in the big-boned frame, and staring at the serene blue eyes: staring.

He felt the impact of incomprehension: the incredulity of eyes that were eyes in every way, that looked at him, and yet could not see him: and he knew in his own way the inertness of that mass that was yet alive; the helplessness. It horrified him.

Suddenly the boy's eyes shifted, his neck craned forward, and he said: 'Don't move, Gramp. There's a spider on your arm.'

He might have told the old man there was a stick of dynamite at his feet, for he was electrified into movement: horror jumped on to his face and he struggled forward in the

94

chair, brushing his clothes wildly and crying: 'Get it off me! Get it off me!'

The boy fell back in amazement at the panic in his grandfather. Then he bustled up to him and said: 'Keep still, and I'll get him. He's on your leg now. He's only a little one.' He slapped at the man's thigh and brushed the spider to the carpet, grinding it with his boot.

'There, he's dead now. I got him.'

He saw the old man collapse in his chair, panting, his face chalky, and his hands shaking; trying to speak.

'I hate them things,' he said huskily.

'Well, he's dead now. I squashed him.'

'Good boy, Joey.' There was relief and pleasure in the old man's voice. He fumbled in his pocket, and the boy's face lit greedily at the jingle of coins. 'Here, here's twenty cents. Go and buy a lolly, that's the boy.'

The boy backed away, delighted, but still astonished at the change that had come over his grandfather.

That evening the old man's daughter said to him: 'You mustn't be giving money to Joe.'

'Only twenty cents,' he said.

'I don't want you to do it, father. He gets enough. Please don't give him any more.'

'All right,' the old man said. He knew the tone in her voice, and he was a prisoner of their stewardship. But he didn't mind giving the boy money. It would perhaps help to bridge the gulf between them, coaxing the boy into fearless friendship; subtly easing away whatever strangeness it was that kept him vaguely remote.

When the boy asked straightout for money, the old man refused him. The boy tried all sorts of subterfuges, but his grandfather would not relent. The boy was broodingly bitter. He had wanted the money especially. He was desperate in his rage.

'Mingy old cow,' he said with hate.

But he affected not to hold any animosity. He had his scheme worked out. He tried it one day when his mother and father were out, and he was alone with the old man in the house.

He suddenly chirruped excitedly: 'Oh, look, Gramp, there's another spider!'

'Where? Where?' cried the old man, disturbance shaking him again.

'It's not near you. It's on the table.'

'Kill it then! Kill it! Don't let it come near me.'

The old man was stumbling out of his chair, the sweat on his face, and panting wheeze coming from his lungs.

'Oh, it's moving across the table now. It's moving. Can spiders smell you, Gramp?'

'Kill it!' screamed the old man. 'Kill it before it drops to the floor.'

The boy watched with hypnotic delight, sensing the power that he wielded: this huge old man subject to him.

'What'll you give me if I kill it?' he breathed.

'Anything, anything! Where is it now?'

'Fifty cents?'

'Yes, yes!'

The boy made a slapping sound. Then he breathed with triumph: 'Now it'll never get you, Gramp. Gimme the fifty cents you said you would. Oh, it's not quite dead. Gimme the fifty cents, Gramp, and I'll squash it.'

The old man's money jingled and spilt in a clinkle out of his hand. The boy gathered up the coins. He put fifty cents in his pocket. Then he tipped the money into the man's hand. The man searched with his fingers and gave the boy the half dollar.

'Thanks, Gramp. Gee, he was a big spider, too. Brown. Hairy legs.'

'Don't tell me about it!' yelled the old man. 'I don't want to hear about it.'

The boy's lips eased apart over his sharp little teeth, and his hand was warm on the two coins in his pocket.

'Crikey, Gramp, I don't know what makes you so scared of spiders.'

'I hate 'em. I hated 'em all my life. I killed every one I saw. There's a lot of spiders in this house.'

'But you needn't worry, Gramp,' the boy said eagerly. 'I'll kill every spider I see, and I'll kill 'em just for you: and you needn't gimme any more than a cent if you don't want to.'

The old man's breathing came stiffly. He waved a hand: 'All right. All right. Leave me alone now. And don't tell your mother I gave you that money.'

'No fear, Gramp. It's just a secret between you and me.'

The boy was very cunning. He didn't try again for a fortnight. He waited until the old man was well on in his pitiable terror. Then he played for the stakes.

'Will you gimme a dollar if I kill it?'

As soon as he said it, he noticed a sudden change in the old man: it was only momentary, but he noticed it. The old man, still gripped in terror, only nodded.

'Gimme the dollar first, then,' the boy said warily.

When he had it, he made a great business of killing the imaginary spider; and he talked a lot, but the old man said nothing. He tried to get some assurance from the old man that he was a good boy and had made the old man happy by killing the spider. But all he got was silence. He went away worried, yet defiant and joyous.

When the boy made another attempt, the old man's lips came tight together and a great anger shook him: 'You dirty little blackmailer. Get out of my sight. Get out, or I'll tell your mother what sort of a son she's got. Get out!' he yelled.

And the boy ran frightened at the wrath in him, but his blood on fire with hate.

The old man shook, not with fear, but with a nervous emotion of unpleasantness. Now he had driven the boy like a wild cat beyond the confines of his friendship, alienated him.

Soon he began to sense the boy's loss about him, and that loss gave the silence chimeras which had never been there before. He began to see spiders as if the boy were pointing them out to him.

In his sleep at night it was not with the terror of an explosion that he woke: the nightmare descent of dusty darkness, and wheels of light spinning in his brain; and noises that were rescuers; and the fresh air meeting his face after the foul stink of the mine; and the great palling abyss of non-independence that had enclosed him until the words of his daughter in his ear gave him knowledge of security and care; four walls and a roof and a watcher.

That was terrible enough. But it was horror that woke him raving: drenched in sweat, crazily slapping at the bedclothes, at the thousand crawling things on his flesh, and spitting out the spiders that crawled down his throat: their bulbous eyes seeking, and their hairy legs spiking his tongue. It was spiders, hundreds of thousands of them, creeping out of the darkness — the real ghosts of his sleep.

And there was one that came, standing on the floor, its body above the bed: black as tar and yellow-streaked, the hair bristling on it, its leg-joints like fractured sticks, its eyes as big as oranges, and its mouth scarlet. And swiftly it worked, netting the bed in silken cables, enmeshing him.

He sobbed and ranted against it: and only a woman's voice full of agitation could assure him that it was driven away, and was no part, had never been a part, of that other darkness.

The old man tried to get on with the boy, speaking kindly to him, coaxing and cajoling, but he couldn't. Yet the boy did not worry him for weeks. He was thus not prepared for the incident when it did happen. He was sitting in the living room again, dozing, when the boy, with a companion, sneaked into the porch, tip-toed to the door, and looked in.

The boy put a finger to his lips and said in a whisper: 'You watch.'

Then he cried in alarm: 'Oh, grandpa, grandpa, look! There's a spider!'

The old man started up, jabbering. Then his face darkened, and he cried out to the boy to get away.

'But, Gramp, it's true! It's true!' piped the boy shrilly.

'You little devil, get when I tell you!'

'All right, don't believe me then. He's on your knee. He's on your knee!'

The old man's mouth opened. Perhaps the boy was right. He slapped at his knee, the panic working up in him, the shock and terror paralysing and activating him.

Then he cried: 'You lying little sweep! God, if I only had my eyes.'

The boy grinned at his companion, who grinned back. Then he took a matchbox from his pocket, and, edging closer to the agitated old man, opened the box and dropped the half-stunned spider on his hand, at the same time stepping back quickly, and yelling: 'He's on your hand! Look out!'

The old man jerked his hand away with a ghastly expression on his face, and terror gurgling in his voice; he smashed his hands, squashing the spider against his knee, and then in a frenzy slapping it off, and rising to his feet, choking and sobbing, groping and blundering.

Then he heard the snickering titter of the boy, and the echo of it from the other, and he knew he was the dupe of a cruel joke. It went like a storm through him, and his hand closed on his walking stick; he went berserk, a scream of fury bursting from his iron lungs, as he swished blindly, the cane singing through space.

The boy fell back in fright, as though caught in the vestiges of a tornado. His companion at the door bolted. The old man slashed and the sound of a globe shattered about his ears; glass and wood swacked and tinkled; and the boy's affrighted cries babbled his whereabouts, pinpointed the target. He was screaming, darting behind chairs, under the table: the cane met his shoulder and cracked against his head, and cracked, and he fell with a sob, fell and crawled towards the door, bloody and stunned to a silence; and sat huddled on the threshold.

And then the old man, aware of the silence, stopped his swishing. He stood upright, staring in horror, gaping. He

99

dropped the cane from his nerveless fingers, and cried out in a distracted voice: 'Joe! Joe!'

The silence shouted back, and it put him on the floor in a craze of fear, down on his hands and knees, groping and crawling, shrieking: 'Joe! Joe! Where are you, Joe?'

And the boy, numb with shock, watching him from the doorway, began to cry deeply with the outrageous self-pity of his experience.

GROWER OF MEN

She was fifty years old now, Ma Wilkins, but she was tall and straight still, like the tree that has fought the same struggles and opposed the same antagonisms as its brothers, but yet rises like a pole into the sky. She was strong and heavy, and her hands were the hands of a man. Her face was full, unlined, brown as autumn leaves; her eyes magnificent and piercing. She always wore the floppy old felt hat that had been her husband's.

When she had the meal ready, she went to the door and called: 'Dave! Laurie! Come on, your tea's up.'

Out of the barn came Dave, a young man, broad, thick. Behind him shambled Laurie in his bare feet, his trousers tattered at the cuffs. He began to run to catch up with his brother. It was a sort of hobbled hop. His jaw hung slackly; his round, huge eyes glistened with a fixed bulging leer. He cried out to Dave to wait for him — cried with a thick, half-intelligible gobble. Dave waited with a patient weariness, and they went in together.

They washed roughly, Dave sluicing himself, Laurie paddling the water up in his face and wetting his shirt; searching for the towel with a blind groping.

When they sat into the table, the woman asked: 'Getting ahead down there?'

Dave screwed up his mouth: 'Ah, the spuds are as poor as hell this year. Take some grading to get anything worthwhile from the seed.'

'They'll keep us going,' Ma said. 'Better crop next year.'

Laurie golloped his soup, spilling it on his shirt and on his bare chest. Ma bounced at him: 'Laurie, where's your napkin? Haven't I told you?'

Laurie baulked guiltily, picked up a cloth from the back of his chair, and fastened it around his neck. He ate like an animal, breaking bread and wolfing it down, picking the meat up with his fingers and wrenching the flesh like a dog with carrion, the gravy running down his chin.

'Wipe your chin, Laurie,' Ma said from time to time.

They ate for a while in silence. Now and then Ma glanced casually at the brown, husky Dave, and then switched her gaze to the boy next to him. A cloud came into her eyes. She could hear the voices that had always been with her since they were children: Never think they were brothers, would you?

So unlike. That one so bright and normal, and the other . . . It lasted only momentarily. She said soberly: 'You going along to see her tonight?'

'Aw, sure thing, Ma,' Dave grinned.

Laurie jerked out: 'I are, too.'

Dave enlarged his grin: 'Now what do you want to do?' he chaffed. 'Pinch my girl from me? You stay here and keep Ma company.'

'Ooomh, I keep Ma company,' gurgled Laurie, strickenly.

'Like you always do,' Dave patted his shoulder. 'Pretty lonely out here in the bush. Never know when somebody might come, and . . .'

'Dave, shut your mouth!' Ma swore like thunder.

Laurie gaped, still looking at Dave, then at Ma, his staring eyes flickering with dull comprehension. Then his mouth twisted. He stood up, his eyes wide. His chest swelled and he pounded it: 'I kill man who touch Ma!' he cried in his half-strangled voice.

Ma went round the table quickly.

'I kill man,' raved Laurie, and taking up his plate tried to bend it like a man with a piece of tin. It cracked and broke. Ma gripped his huge shoulders and screamed at Dave: 'See what you've done now, blast you! Why don't you get to hell out of here with that talk? You ought to know better.'

Dave bit his lip: 'Ah, he gets upset over nothing. I just thought . . .'

'Well, don't think! Come on, Laurie . . . there's no one coming here. Look, Laurie, listen to me . . .'

She tried to coax him, but he kept on fuming and raving.

Suddenly she clouted him hard across the mouth, and shouted terribly: 'Shut up! You hear me? Shut up!'

The command acted instantly on the demented man. He fell back in his chair abruptly quiet, just staring, the storm in him dying. Ma left him. She went into the kitchen. Dave followed her: 'You're not mad at me, are you, Ma? You know he can't come.'

'I thought you might stay home one night. You've been seeing her every night since she came here.'

'Two weeks, that's all,' Dave flared. 'And it's my business, ain't it?'

Ma looked calmly at him: 'I understand how it is, but Dave, he likes you. He likes to play cards with you. Every night you're gone he asks me why you don't play cards with him any more.'

'Aw hell, Ma, have some sense. I don't want to play cards when I've got a girl to go to. He's with me all day, like a dog. It gets on my goat.'

'Better go if you're going,' she said. 'It's all right with me, Dave.'

Half-resentful, Dave cleaned up and dressed. Laurie was still sitting dumbly in the chair when he came out of his room. Dave said to him: 'Maybe one night later on I'll take you with

103

me.' Panicky delight transformed Laurie's face, and he nodded. Dave called out goodnight to Ma, washing up, and left.

Laurie shambled in and took the tea towel. Ma looked at him, felt that behind his deep silence his mind was at grips with some thought. Her eyes narrowed.

'He'll take you one night, he said, didn't he?'

Laurie nodded joyfully: 'Ooomh, I go, too, Dave say.'

The woman looked at him. She knew what he was wondering: what his brain refused to unravel. He was puzzled by Dave's behaviour ever since the new people had come. He couldn't understand why Dave had forgone his nights of cards and dominoes to go and see a girl. He felt he was being slighted.

'I never go nowhere, Ma,' he said.

'You don't want to go anywhere.'

'Dave goes to town Saturday. He goes out in the night. I go, too. Maybe you get me a girl, Ma.'

'Don't talk rubbish!' she snapped, half-alarmed at the thought.

Then she knew it was Laurie's way of wanting to do the same things as Dave, things that must be refused him. It had always been like that. School, for instance. School was a place of learning and normal behaviour to Dave, but to Laurie it was a nightmare of tortuous unintelligibility and malicious cruelties, of sadistic japes and horrible pity that conceived him as beyond and alien to the others, as if he had never been born of a woman but of a monster. School was the force that drove her to shield him as with a cloak from eyes and mouths, and protect him from the terrors and horrors of civilization. Yet she had borne him as she had borne Dave.

She thought of Laurie as a baby. He was glozed over by admiring people just as his brother was. People never froze from him then. They never laughed, or tormented him, or crossed to the other footpath when they saw him coming. And they grew, both of them, but one went wrong.

'You'll have no girl,' Ma said. 'Girls are not good for some men, and you're one of them. Besides, would you be leaving me every night, too?'

Laurie gazed at her. Slowly, his head nodded; 'I stay with you, Ma. I stay here.'

When they went into the dining room, he asked her if she would play cards with him. She told him she wanted to read. He got out the cards and began to play solitaire. For a while she watched him, his intent face, his scruffy hair, his delight. Then she put her glasses on and took up the paper . . . In a little while he came round to her and sat on the floor at her feet.

'Ma?'

'Yes?'

'You tell me, Ma, where I come from.'

'I've told you, Laurie, time and time again.'

'You tell me some more, Ma.'

She put the paper down with a patient sigh: 'Well, you came from me. You came from me when it was a cold . . .'

'No, no, Ma!' he cried. 'You tell about the tree and the soil . . .' His thick tongue lolloped around in his mouth. 'You tell about the tree . . .'

She looked at him. She had told him a thousand times. He always came back to hear the story again. He either forgot it, or liked to hear it repeated. She never forgot the first time he had asked her the question. It was then that she had framed the mode of her enlightenment, shaped the answer to his understanding.

She said: 'You tell me, Laurie.'

He began in a babble: 'I are a tree, and I growed up from a little tree. The soil is . . . is . . .'

'Rich,' she helped him.

He shook his head: 'No, Ma — you tell about the soil and the tree.'

'All right. Be still then.'

He stared into her face as she spoke, his mouth open, his eyes glossy.

'Well,' she began . . . 'well, at first you were nothing. Your father had no thought of you. Neither did I, your mother. Then I said one night: We should have a child, and that was you, just as a desire — like when you want a horse or a dog that you see. So it was agreed. You know the little seeds out there on the kitchen shelf? You know you have seen me take them and put them in the soil. And you have seen sunflowers come up where I planted one lot and trees where I planted another.'

Like a child, Laurie nodded eagerly and joyfully.

'You have not seen sunflowers come up in place of trees, have you? They spring from different seeds, that's why. Well, the seed of your father was different to both of these again. From your father's seed grew flesh and blood. Your father put his seed in me, and I was the soil it grew in. It grew in me, that seed, like the seed in the ground. And it was in darkness like the earth for a long time, months, but it was growing all the time, and coming out of the darkness into the light.

'For, just as the earth is a grower of flowers and trees and vegetables, so too, is a woman a grower of men; and I grew you and Dave. And then you were born. But being born, Laurie, is like this: You remember when we took those little green apple trees and transplanted them? Well, that's what birth means. You were taken from me, the soil of your body and your life, and transplanted in the world. The world became the soil in which you lived, then, and developed, just like the trees that grow big and strong in the sun and the air. And so you are what you are today. You are a man.'

'But . . . Dave and me are different.'

'Different, yes, because no two seeds are alike. But your father and I made you no different. You came into me as Dave came, and spent the same time in me, and you came out the same way.'

He nodded with a combination of blankness and understanding. She didn't go on, voicing the consecutive thoughts in her mind: Something happened in the transplanting, the soil of the world, or perhaps in your generation before you. But you're no less near to me because of that, no matter how many shun you. You're just the same as if you were curled up inside me and I didn't know whether you were Laurie or David. It was just some cruel, unfair, terrible thing that happened to make you not as other men: and the cruellest thing about it is that you had nothing to do with it. You didn't even ask to be born. But you're penalized for it as if you did something bad, as if you committed a sin, as if it was your fault.

She said no more.

Laurie stared with a glowing triumph in his eyes: 'I are a tree and I come from my mother!' He said this over and over again in a crescendo of hysterical delight. She touched his arm and he quietened. He became sober. Ma looked at him. Next week he would come back and ask to be told the story again.

She saw his lips moving, his mouth working in a hideous and pathetic distortion, striving to make some utterance. Patiently, she coaxed him, waiting for the words to come. He said: 'The tree belongs to the grower, Ma. I belong to you. I are your tree, and so are Dave. Your tree, too.'

She was surprised. He had never said that before. It was a thought she did not think him capable of evolving.

'Yes, the tree belongs to the grower,' she said; 'and the grower must look after it. But the grower, Laurie, does not interfere with the freedom of the tree where it would be against reason to do so. The tree grows, and the grower does not measure the space of the air it must grow in. He does not say: You must not expand so much. Not unless he has proper cause. He does not wish its colour to be different, or say against the size of its limbs. Whatever he does to the tree must be for its own good. Just so with you that grew in me. I would not interfere with your ways of freedom where it was wrong to do so. Nor with Dave's, either . . .'

She saw that he did not even half-understand this, but she didn't bother to explain. He would chew it over in his mind and come back again. She yawned, and said she was going to bed. He didn't say anything, mumbled when she said goodnight, and then he was alone. He got up and put the lamp out and sauntered into his room. He got into bed, his head twisted towards the window, his eyes staring at the stars.

Ma was up at half-past four. She had their breakfast ready when they got up. She went down and fed the pigs and fowls.

It was only a small holding, and they made only a living from it. Last year the corn was a bad price, and this year the potatoes had come to nothing. But she knew there would be a year of plenty sometime. The fields were fallowing, stung by the frosts, enriched by sun and air.

When she came inside again, Dave said: 'Had a great time at Lampson's last night, Ma. Good scout that old Lampson. Brought out the wine and treated me. Said he'd like to meet you sometime.'

'He knows where I am,' said Ma with disinterest.

'He's a damn good neighbour to have,' Dave told her, prickling slightly.

'Has he got fowls — and pigs, and potaters, Dave?' Laurie jerked out.

'Too right he has. And horses and cows, too. He's looking for men he's got so much work. He wants a boundary rider for his station at Walgett. Yeah, another big homestead. Got a son in charge of that, but wants a boundary rider. Offered the job to me.'

Ma looked at Dave: 'What'd you say?'

Dave grinned: 'Aw, I couldn't take it, Ma. I've got my hands full here.'

'Take it if you want to,' Ma said.

'No,' said Dave. 'I'm sticking around here.'

She was relieved.

For three weeks Dave went over every night to see Peggy Lampson, and on Sundays they went for an outing together. Laurie asked each time if he could go, reminding Dave of his promise, but Dave always put him off, saying the time wasn't right yet or that he had something special to say, or that he wanted Laurie to get a new shirt first. Ma saw the transparency of these excuses, but Laurie didn't. He just caught on to the glamorous prospect, and became excited and exuberant.

One Sunday, after lunch, Ma was sitting on the veranda reading a magazine when Laurie ambled round and sat on the step. She saw his restlessness. He was whittling a potato, carving it, whittling it. She said: 'You going to set some traps tonight?'

He looked up sharply: 'But you tell me no. You say, Laurie, don't you set no more traps.'

'Come here.'

He shambled over to her, stroked his quiff of hair back, and stood beside her looking into her face. 'Yes, Ma,' he nodded.

'Would you like to?' she asked.

His eyes lit: 'Set some more traps and catch some rabbits?'

She nodded and watched him. His face shone with delight, and he rubbed his hands with excitement. He turned to make for the shed. She called after him, and he stood with a sudden impingement of dismay on his face as though he feared she would revoke her permission.

She said: 'I'll let you go and set some traps today if you promise to be back before sundown.'

He nodded eagerly: 'Before sundown.'

'Not like last time, Laurie, when you stayed away till late. I don't want to have to go looking for you with a lantern this time. Remember?'

'Before sundown, Ma,' he said lolloping to the shed.

She remembered coming upon him sitting under a rock with joy rigid on his face. It was one o'clock in the morning. Twenty yards from him was a rabbit warren where he had set some of his traps. As she faced him brittle-eyed, he pointed jubilantly at three pelts wet and blood-smeared beside him. Almost at the same instant a trap clacked and the piercing squeal of a rabbit came in waves of terror, electrifying him into action. He scrambled over the ground into the darkness, and she followed in time to see the animal wrenched from the trap, its broken leg with the peeling fur still between the serrated jaws. She saw him stretch the rabbit's neck and hold its convulsing body by the single hind leg. Its bolting eyes were like his, only his were alive with a black fire.

'Ma,' he cried. 'You stay with me. We catch more rabbits.' He bent down and reset the trap, sprinkling dirt over the plate until all was as the earth around. 'We catch more rabbits, plenty rabbits, Ma.'

'Get your stuff.'

'I only want to catch rabbits. I do no bad.'

'You hear me, Laurie.'

He obeyed currishly, springing the traps, tossing them over his shoulder and following her silently back to the house.

Now he came out of the shed with his traps, muttering excitedly to himself. Ma called him over to her. She said: 'The last time, Laurie — remember we had a talk when we came home. I told you why you could never go rabbiting again and why I brought you home.'

He nodded, rushing out his knowledge: 'Before sundown, Ma. I be home.'

'If you are,' she said: 'I might let you go again sometime.'

She watched him hastening away; and she felt satisfied that she had made him happy.

Laurie sauntered along the gully, stopping to pick berries and rush them into his mouth. He went up over the naked hills, and struck out across an arid watercourse. Crows cawed harshly, flopping away from a heap of dead wool. He went up to the sheep and stared at the clots of maggots writhing and crawling in stinking fascicles on the end of a stick. He gathered up a tatter of rotten flesh alive with them and dropped it on to an ant bed. He became wildly excited when the bed swarmed with a black motion as the colony attacked the trespasser.

He felt as though he had been let out of a cage after a long imprisonment.

To the south he saw the warren on a saddle of yellow and red clay and he stumbled quickly towards it. Climbing a small ridge he stopped. Down at the bottom of the gentle slope he saw Dave and Peggy Lampson on their horses, riding side by side, and talking. The horses stopped and Dave leant over and kissed the girl.

'Dave's girl,' breathed Laurie, goggle-eyed and delighted. He began to shout and bolt hobbling towards them.

Dave turned his head, staring at the wild shambling figure, distressed. He darted a look at the girl. She was intrigued.

He said: 'Come on, Peg. Let's get away from here.'

Laurie waved strickenly and yelled: 'Dave! Dave . . .'

Peggy Lampson said: 'Who is it, Dave?'

Then Laurie was there, gape-eyed and stuttering thick unintelligible speech. Dave saw a slight curious horror on the girl's face. He felt sick in his belly.

His eyes slitted. 'What are you doing here?' His voice was cold with a curbed anger.

Laurie panted, staring at Peggy Lampson, his head nodding.

'Go on home,' Dave said. 'Go on when I tell you.'

Laurie looked aghast: 'No, Dave,' he cried. 'Ma, she tell me I set traps. Catch rabbits. Ma say.'

Dave, under the urge of his discomfort sought relief in a furious rage. He wanted to get off his horse and scruff his brother, slap his face, and thrust him away. His passion craved to exact that punishment. But he was afraid Peggy might take some exception to the brutality of his character.

He gave an unsure laugh, and tried to humour Laurie: 'All right, go and set your traps then. I'll be looking forward to some rabbit stew tomorrow. Catch me a nice fat tender bunny.'

'Yes, Dave, I catch you one,' Laurie nodded, joyfully. He looked at the girl: 'And you too. I catch you a bunny.'

'I'd like that,' said Peggy Lampson, only her lips smiling. 'What's your name,' she added.

'Laurie.'

Dave tightened his mouth.

Laurie burbled on: 'Dave tell you about me? I are Dave's brother. Dave say I come and see you some time when I get some new clothes. I come and see you at your place.'

The girl smiled artificially, looked mystified at Dave: 'Your brother?' she said.

Dave did not answer her. His face was pale, blaze-eyed. He slapped his horse. 'I'll see you later, Laurie,' he said. 'Come on, Peggy.'

Peggy followed.

Laurie shrieked happily: 'Goodbye Dave. Goodbye, lady.'

He looked after them cantering away, and went off to set his traps.

Just after sundown Dave returned. He strode into the room where Ma was setting the table, and said quietly: 'Where is he?' She saw the white of his face, the bewildering passion of rage in his eyes.

'Dave, what's the matter?'

'Laurie. Where is he?' Dave fumed. Then he heard the shuffling feet in the kitchen and Laurie came in, grinning when he saw Dave. Dave pulled the thick plaited belt from around his waist, and Laurie squealed as he came towards him. He took one swish across the shoulders, turned and ran out and down towards the barn. Dave followed him, stung to a greater need to spend his fury on his brother.

When Ma got to the barn, Dave was yelling: 'Come down here. I'll teach you to keep away from me.'

Laurie in a corner on a row of potatoes stared in terror. He shrilled as Dave sprang on to the bags and scrambled towards him.

Ma grabbed Dave, pulled him back with all her strength, struck him across the face, and tore the belt from his hands: 'What's come over you?' she cried. 'Are you mad?' She cried at his sober silence: 'If there's anything Laurie's to be punished for I'll do it. You hear.'

'You now what you want to do then,' cried Dave bitterly.

'You want to take him into the bush and put a bullet in him!'

'What's he done to you?'

'I wish to Christ he'd never been born,' Dave said.

'Dave, what are you saying.'

She stood there, shocked; though she believed it was only the rage and disappointment about something that was talking in Dave. It wasn't his belief. She had to straighten it out. She told Laurie to go inside. Puzzled and scared, he scrambled down and loped away.

'Now what happened, Dave?'

'What happened? He came up to us out there, that's all. Simpering and gibbering. I never felt so sick in all my life.'

'She saw him?'

Dave nodded: 'And I'm ashamed. Ashamed. It's a terrible thing for a man to have to lie about his own brother.'

'What do you mean?' she asked.

'I couldn't tell her he was my brother, could I? I had to lie to her. Tell her he wasn't one of us. Only adopted.'

'It was my fault, Dave. I let him go off. I didn't know. And how did you expect him to know any better? You know Laurie, as well as I know him.'

'I know him all right. That's the trouble. He's got to be hidden away, kept in a cage, on a chain. The whole family suffers because of him. I knew that the day Dad was killed.'

She had a flash of her husband in the storm struck dead by lightning, the rescuers come upon him to find a drenched and sobbing animal that was Laurie lying across him, refusing dog-like to let anyone come near him: and how afterwards Laurie stood laughing hysterically in his shock and grief.

She sat down beside Dave. 'I'm sorry it happened, son. I don't blame you for lying. It was the best thing you could do. But don't blame Laurie for what he did.'

Dave knew he couldn't blame Laurie. He saw the wisdom of his mother's words. But he wasn't going to back down overtly. She pacified him and they all ate at the table without a word. After tea, Laurie got the dominoes out.

With a shrug, Dave said: 'Come on, I'll give you a game.'

Laurie bustled delightedly, feeling, as always, nothing but affection for his brother.

Ma was pleased; she knew the incident was finished between them.

Then one Saturday evening four months later, Dave came in about six. Ma saw his flushed face, his bright eyes. His speech was quick and eager: 'Well, Ma, you're about to get a daughter-in-law. Peggy's promised to marry me. She's going to be my wife.'

He waited, smiling, expecting Ma to be glad. But her face showed no emotion, even of interest.

Dave said: 'Well, what's wrong? Don't you like it?'

The woman put a hand to her temple. Her lips quivered faintly: 'You surprised me Dave. I never thought . . .'

'I only asked her today. She's a great girl, Ma. She'll make a good wife.'

Ma was silent, disappointed, antagonized by a trespassing anxiety, but she showed nothing of it on her face: 'When will you be married?'

'About a fortnight. Lampson says that job's still open at Walgett, but he said he can use me here, too. I like the Walgett job, though, Ma, and I think I'll take it. It's all right with you, ain't it?'

She said soberly: 'What matter if it wasn't? You'd still go ahead. But, yes, Dave, it's all right.'

Laurie, who had been looking from one to the other of them, now said: 'You don't go away, Dave?'

Dave explained with a laugh: 'When a man gets married, Laurie, he can't live with his mother. He lives with his girl, his wife. I've got to go away, yes, but I'll be back to see you now and then. And I'll write . . .'

'No!' cried Laurie, his face working in a panic. 'You don't go away.'

'Tell him, will you, Ma?'

'Laurie, Dave's got to go away,' Ma said. 'He can't live here any more.'

Laurie shook his head wildly; his speech was thicker than usual: 'No! No.! This girl do not own Dave. You own him.' He walked over to Dave, who watched with a slight wary puzzlement. 'Ma growed you. You Ma's tree. You belong to Ma.'

'What are you talking about?'

Laurie thrust out his hands and gripped Dave's biceps. His voice rose: 'You like me. You belong to Ma. You Ma's tree. She growed you.' He started to shake Dave, as if to force the fact into his mind. Dave's quick anger was tempted. He tried to shake the hands off, but they were like steel clamps.

'Get your hands off me,' he whipped out. What the hell do you think you're doing?'

'You Ma's tree,' mouthed Laurie.

'Get your bloody hands off me or I'll swipe you one!'

Ma grabbed one of Laurie's arms: 'Stop it. Take your hands off Dave.'

'But Dave . . .'

'Take your hands off him!' Ma shouted. Laurie's hands fell away. His jaw hung slackly. He was subdued by her mastery.

'What crazy idea's got into him?' cried Dave. 'You're going to be a brother-in-law. Don't you know that? You can come to the wedding.'

'Shut up, Dave,' Ma said, 'you know he can't go to any wedding. You know why you never took him over to Lampson's as you promised. So do I. I understand. I don't blame you, but I don't want you leading him on. See?'

'Okay,' said Dave.

Laurie cried: 'I kill this girl that take you from Ma.'

'You hold your tongue, Laurie, and stop that talk. Dave is right. He loves this girl, and he has the right to go away if he wants to. You don't let me hear you talk like that again.'

'No, nor me, either,' Dave muttered.

'Now everything's all right,' said Ma, pacifically. 'I want no bad blood between you boys.'

Dave broke into a quick grin: 'There's nothing like that, Ma.

Well, they're going to the pictures tonight. I'm going with them, so I'll just get a bit of tea into me and get moving.'

After tea Ma was in the kitchen, and Laurie sat in the dining room, silent. In a while the background noise of crockery ceased in his brain. He got up and walked to the door. Ma was standing still, holding a handkerchief to her nose. Laurie heard her sniffle slightly. Alarm and bewilderment came on his face. He went towards her. She heard him, then, and made a quick dab at her eyes, tucking the handkerchief away and going on with the dishes.

'Ma, you cry about Dave .'

'No, Laurie,' she said. 'It's all right.'

'She take Dave away from you.' His glassy eyes rounded. 'She steal Dave. You tell about the rabbit and the bandicoot . . . they come and steal the little plants and you shoot them. You tell me that, Ma, you tell me that. This girl steal Dave, your tree that you growed, and . . .'

'Laurie, I tell you it's all right. Go and play cards. I'll wipe these up tonight.'

'I hate this girl that steal Dave from you. I hate this girl . . .'

'You mind your own business. We can manage without Dave, and if this makes him happy it is a good thing. Now go on Laurie, you forget all about it. I said it's all right, and it is all right.'

Laurie went out, mechanically took the cards and placed them on the table. But he wasn't interested in them. He watched his mother come in and take up a a paper and read. He said nothing. She mentioned a few news items and commented on them. Laurie sensed, rather than reasoned, the dilaceration that had taken place in her life. It made him feel more bitter against the Lampson girl. Incapable of reason and logic, he felt only the force of primitive emotions, hate, and protectiveness, and conscionable righteousness.

He said: 'If this girl never come here Dave would not go away.'

Immersed in the paper, she refused to answer him. He

sensed that she wanted to say nothing more about it. She went to bed, and he soon after. He waited, lying awake, until Dave came in about midnight. He heard the door lock, his boots on the boards; then he was in the room, undressing in the dark, lying in bed.

Hot tears oozed out of Laurie's eyes. He was thinking of the room when Dave was not in it, but gone away.

Next morning Dave came in from the barn after sewing up a few bags, and Ma said: 'Think we'll get any rain out of this?'

'Well, the wind's in the right quarter. But you know what it's like, Ma. Comes up like this, black as thunder, and not a drop. Just blows over.'

'Yes, I know. What's Laurie doing?'

'He's gone shooting; ain't he?'

Ma looked up sharply: 'Shooting? When? I never told him he could go shooting.'

'Well, he hasn't been with me. I seen him going off about five minutes ago with a rifle.'

The colour drained out of Ma's face, and a look of dread came there. Dave saw this; he prickled with a sense of danger.

'God Almighty!' he exclaimed, and his face went white. 'You mean . . .?' He suddenly turned and went to the gun rack. 'The bloody lunatic! I'll kill him.'

She was busy then pulling her apron off. 'You stay here. I'll get him.'

'No, I'm going.'

'You stay here, Dave,' she ordered. 'I'll get him, I tell you. Give me that rifle.'

Dave stood white, unmoving, only his eyes blazing with anger and fear. 'By God, if he's done anything to her I swear I'll kill him stone dead.'

'Don't worry. I'll bring him back. Now you stay here.'

She went fast against the wind, under the louring sky. Her mind raced. She feared what he might do. She feared what they might do to him: a man come upon them with a rifle and a crazy gabble about trees and soil, a language that was his and alien to them: a seeming lunatic with threats and hate in his eyes. And she could see the police taking the man and punishing him for what he believed was right doing, as if they condoned stealing and repudiated the principles of the tree and the soil.

She ploughed quickly across the rough paddock, got through the fence and made south. She knew that with his start on her she must cut the distance to catch him. The only short cut lay to the south. He might have taken that: he might have taken the road. She scrambled to the top of a hill and scanned the countryside, peering among the bunched trees and over the bare flats. At first she saw nothing moving. Then he appeared from behind the trees six hundred yards to her left. He was walking along the road.

Her mind worked quickly. If she took a parallel route and then cut in to the left she could head him off. She ran and stumbled, panting. Her heart galloped and she felt the blood pound in her temples. But she was strong and enduring. She hurried through a belt of trees, and then cut in, taking a way that led her to a bend in the road.

Panting harshly, she knew that he was not ahead of her; and then she saw him shambling along, the rifle down like his head, just going towards his inexorable purpose. She was hidden till he rounded the bend.

Then she cried: 'Laurie!'

He stopped, stood stock-still and stared as though he had been caught in a guilty act.

'Turn back, Laurie,' she said.

His mouth began to work and his head to nod; a flash of hateful fury fired his eyes: 'I . . . I kill that girl, Ma.'

'You heard me, Laurie.' Her voice was steady. 'Give me that rifle and go back home.'

'No!' he cried in defiance; like an animal in sudden rebellion, maddened by his frustration. 'You go back, Ma. You go back!'

She raised her rifle, pointing the barrel at his chest: 'Laurie, listen to me. You remember that dog old Adams used to have. You remember how it wanted its way. It ran about howling, foam dripping from its mouth, and it bit you and tried to bite me. What'd they do to it? They shot it, didn't they, Laurie? You know why, Laurie, don't you? It was a mad dog. It wanted to bite and kill people. It had some idea people were going to hurt it, or had hurt it. You always have to shoot a dog when it gets like that, Laurie.'

She saw his eyes go hideously round and stare, and some of the colour paled in his face. She held him with her eyes, the gun unwaveringly pointed towards him.

'You saw that dog lie dead when Adams shot it. And you saw Adams come over with his head down, and you heard him say: "I liked that dog; but there was nothing else I could do." Sometimes, Laurie, men get like that dog, and you have to shoot them, though you don't want to.'

She saw the hate and bafflement in his face, and she thought it might overpower him, cause him to insurrect against her and go on.

She said no more.

She waited.

Then she saw his shoulders slump; and his rifle fell in the dust. He stood there stricken, like an automaton, ready for her directions.

She lowered her rifle and picked up his. Then she said: 'We'll go back, Laurie.'

He turned and stumbled off, she beside him. They went across the field and towards the house. Dave was standing at the door, his fists clenched. As they came up, he stepped forward, and with a savage curse struck his brother in the mouth, knocking him to the ground.

'You ought to have that loony bastard put away,' he cried in a high-pitched voice that spoke of his anxiety and relief. 'I'm sick of him. I'm sick of this place. I'm going to pack my things and get out of it right away. I'm fed up.'

He tore into the house. Ma helped Laurie. There was a little trickle of blood at the corner of his mouth. He was crying. Dave didn't take long. He came out with his belongings stuffed in a sugar bag. His eyes were blazing. He left without a word, and they watched him going in the direction of Lampson's.

Laurie stood behind looking over Ma's shoulder. There was no coldness in the woman's eyes; only knowledge of inevitability. She felt the hot breath of Laurie on her neck. She was suddenly pleased that he was what he was: for it bound him to her; it was her security against empty years, forgotten isolation, loneliness.

'Laurie,' she said. 'You don't understand, do you? But you were going to do a terrible thing today. I know what you think and it's true. I am the soil that grew you and Dave. You are a tree and Dave is a tree.'

She looked into his eyes, seeing there the simplicity of her analogies to his understanding.

'But that girl did not steal Dave. She is like the wind, the rain, the storm that comes with lightning. You have seen the tree in a storm, Laurie: how it throws its head about and creaks in the earth. And we can't stop the storm. It has a right to come, just as the tree has a right to grow. And you have seen the branches fall in the high wind, tear and break away, and sometimes the lightning has struck, and taken the tree dead to the ground.'

'So it is with Dave, Laurie, and you and me. We can do nothing, and we don't want to do anything. When a tree goes we do not harm the storm. We just go on living like the other trees that are left. For a while we are shaken: then we find we are all right again.'

She looked at him: 'I have you, Laurie, and you have me. You stay with me Laurie.'

Laurie nodded in helpless faith.

'I stay with you, Ma,' he said.

A LITTLE WHILE AGO

A little while ago he came up from the back paddock. He came up with the bucket in his hand. Not an hour ago. The sun was on the chimney. Now the sun is gone. And he's in there lying down.

It's a thing to make you dumb. He had the fire in his eyes. They are dull like shells now.

You don't think of a great strong man like that lying down, lying still. In sleep he was not even quiet. All through him there was life. It rumbled from his open mouth. It pulsed in his temples. His chest rose and fell with the great tides of his breathing. If you walked the room you felt that his nerves were aware of your movements, following you like the head of a mantis.

Always with me it's been a little while ago. It is only a little while ago I met him at Tihema and married him. How do I know why? Was it lying awake in the night thinking of the wide world and nowhere anybody to worry about me?

He saw me in the room making his bed, and he told me I was the best-looker he ever saw. He came back to the pub in the afternoon and gave me a bracelet. He told me he would see me when he came into town again the next week, and he said he would take me to the races if I could get the half day off.

I said nothing, but I thought about him. He walked around my mind. He wouldn't leave it. He had a strong face dark with the sun. His shoulders were striking. Even the ruggedness was in his voice. He had eyes like chips of a glass, and sometimes they looked cruel and sometimes soft in the way of a cat. His jaws were faintly sooted with black whiskers shaved to the skin. I thought of nobody else all the week. When he came in I wanted to see him. I was glad. It could have been such a disappointment. I could have felt such a fool.

He took me to the races. He told me the names of horses and I backed them. He gave me the money to back them with. When they won I gave him the winnings, but he wanted me to share with him. I didn't want to, but he made me take half. He had many drinks at the booth. He was happy. I was happy, too.

That night he asked me to come to his room. I wasn't going, but I went. He had a bottle of wine. He stood up. He didn't say a word. He came close to me, looking at me, and I had to look away. He kissed me and he wanted to touch me; he tried to touch me, but I told him not to. I told him not to. I should have gone out of the room, but I didn't want to go.

'How old are you?' he said.

I said: 'Sixteen.'

He stood back from me and kept looking up and down, and nodding his head.

'You're the prettiest shape I've ever seen,' he said. 'White or brown.' He kept looking at me. 'What a waste, not to let me see you properly.'

I said: 'What do you mean?'

He came over to me slowly, smiling. 'What are you looking scared like that for? I'm not going to hurt you.'

He put his big hands on my shoulders. The fingers dug into my flesh, but there was no pain, only excitement. He wanted me to take off my clothes.

I said no, I wouldn't, and pulled away from him.

'Ah, come on now,' he said. 'Be nice. Just your dress then.'

But I told him no. I ran to the door and looked back at him. I told him he was drunk and disgusting. I saw the look on his face and I won't forget it. I went to my room, but he might as well have been there. I cried for the look on his face. I couldn't get the sight of him out of my mind. He was everywhere in the darkness, wherever I looked. If he had been there in the flesh I would have done what he wanted.

In the morning he came to me and said he was sorry. He asked me to forgive him. I did. It was easy. I don't know what I would have done if he hadn't come.

Like every half-caste I've always wanted to marry a white man; yet only three weeks later I married him, that big Maori. He took me to the house he built on the poor hard land. It was full of a man who had lived a long time alone. He had gathered things. He had brought home things. I was one more thing to be added to them all. Like them, I had a use for him. I didn't know it then, but I knew it soon.

I got no love or kindness. I tried not to mind that. I thought they might come. But I got no respect, either, and I minded that. It went on for months, and I became even less to him. I was nothing. He hardly talked to me. He only wanted me sometimes. He had his moods and I was caught up in them. He hit me. And I did nothing to make him hit me. His tongue was foul. What did I do to make it foul?

Then I understood something. I thought I did, anyway. He wanted something from life and he didn't get it. I wanted something, too. I didn't get it, either. He was still eaten by loneliness. And so was I. Neither of us had got rid of it.

When I understood this I pitied him. I despised myself for failing to give him whatever he wanted from life and I tried to do better. I tried hard. I told him I understood. I hoped it would make him pity me, and make him do better, too, so that we could meet halfway and make a go of it. But he didn't seem to feel or think that way. He only got worse.

I thought: What does he want? Does he know himself? Some people don't. They go through life searching till they die, and they die without ever finding what they wanted because they never knew what it was they did want. It may be that he knows quite well what he wants, happiness, contentment, but he doesn't know how to get these things; and he tries one way after another and as all of them fail he is only made more lonely and disappointed, more bitter.

He faulted me in everything I did. When the rain hung off and the land was parched I was to blame. I was to blame when the blight came on the crops; when the kerosene ran out in the lamps and there was no more; when the chill sickened him and the phone got out of order. For a thousand things the blame was mine.

I used to put on the wireless. I listened to the music. I saw quiet waters and sunlight breaking through the trees like golden dust. I heard the crash of dark seas and I saw the anchored rocks. And when I thought about it, it seemed that I was like that peaceful backwater and he was like the booming violent waters that broke on the rocks and slowly ground them away.

When he went down in the paddock, when I had the house to myself, I could sing then sometimes. I could be sorry for him. I could wish for the strength and the knowledge to find a way out for us, to make him happy. When he came up from the paddock I shivered. I watched through the window to see his face. I waited for him to come in and trembled in wait for the words. He might be silent or he might be harsh.

One night when the rage took him he told me I could clear out. He said he had had enough of me.

'You hate me,' he said. 'You hate this place and you hate this land. I can see it in your face every day. I don't like seeing it. And I don't want to see it no more. Get your things and get out.'

I told him he was wrong. I told him I wanted to lie with him and be his wife. But he wouldn't listen. I told him we ought to go away somewhere else and start a fresh life in a new place where the earth was kinder and the skies less hopeless. But he roared me down. I told him I wanted him and he wanted me. And if we had a change it would all be different; it would work out if we tried. But he struck me across the mouth with the back of his hand and the blood gushed from my mouth.

'You white man's bastard,' he said. 'You're like a cur dog under a man's feet. You give me nothing but misery. All you do is get in the way. All the time. I want no part of you any more.'

He meant it, and I knew this was the end. Not only had I not given him the happiness he wanted, but in his mind I was the cause of his unhappiness. It had to be something and I was it.

But he didn't have to say that. He didn't have to put that terrible feeling in me of not belonging to anyone. He wasn't going to throw me away like an old broken rabbit trap, like a tin to rust on a dump of tins. I had so much to give someone, and I wanted to give it, but that man wasted me. There is nothing I wouldn't do for a man who cherished me. But he took what he wanted of me and it was gone forever; and it could have been given to someone who deserved it and hungered for it and loved it, and loved the person who gave it, but now it was gone.

And I knew I would go, because I had come to the end of my believing and hoping there would be a change, a way of life for us together. Why had I stayed so long with this man when I could have left him? That's why, because I wanted him, and I wanted him to want me, and I never gave up hope.

But I didn't go. I didn't go, because he grabbed my hand and wrenched the bracelet off my wrist, the bracelet he gave me, and twirled it around on his finger and said: 'This'll do for the next one.'

That's why I didn't go. That's why I hung on for a week, and looked at him in sleep; woke early in the morning and looked at him; walked up to the bedside when he dozed with fatigue and watched him and walked away and back again, afraid of the terror, calmed as it was, and afraid of the temptation of that calm.

And now it's happened.

He came up from the paddock and his mood was savage. He told me to get to hell. He wouldn't give me another chance. He threw out my bags and my things. He hit me with the bucket. He cut my face. He went in and dropped on the bed. He stretched out and he went to sleep.

I took the rifle and I stood and watched by his bedside — and slowly his eyes opened. One minute he was lying there on the bed. When I pulled the trigger his arms flung themselves about, he rolled over and he fell on the floor. I shot him again and that was all.

In the house it was alive, this thing that told me to do it. There was hate and fear. There is emptiness now, like a plain under the sun. And it's all been so swift, the change, everything. It's hard to believe it's true.

I didn't want to kill him. But I had to show him I wasn't dirt. More than that, I had to show myself I wasn't dirt.

You came so quickly, too. It's not long since I rang. I suppose I'll have to go with you. What'll they do to me, sergeant? Will they hang me? I'm young. I'm only seventeen. Seems no time since I went to the races. Only a little while ago.

MY BROTHER JOHNNY

*H*ow can I tell you this story? How can I make you believe it? He wasn't different from any other kid right up to the time he was eight. He just went suddenly. And I didn't think he was my brother any longer. He was like a stranger for the first year, till he got used to us. The old man died; he was a sawyer and the saw ripped his belly open, and he died there at the timberyard. We moved then from the city to the country, and I started work in a grocery store. I was only twelve, but I had to work. The old lady took in washing, and went up to clean the church three days a week.

She gave Johnny his lessons at home, but he didn't take in much. He just ate and slept and prowled around the yard in a silent way. He used to punch beetles and spiders against the grass, and look up triumphantly, snorting through his dilated nostrils.

Sometimes he'd grab me and try to wrestle with me. The first time I thought I could beat him easily. But he surprised me. His body was like iron. He clutched and hugged like steel pincers. He could throw me every time, and I couldn't move under him.

He began to pull palings from the front fence. He'd stand

there, and when someone passed he'd yank a paling out with ease. Some of the town kids stopped to talk to him. Johnny talked slowly; but the words came in a jumble of sound when he was excited. The kids used to get him exhibiting his strength. They brought him horseshoes, and had bets among themselves that he couldn't twist them. They watched him snap electric flex.

They brought physical culture books to him; filled with pictures of muscled men, fighters and weightlifters.

Johnny believed everything the kids said about him; he became upset at some of the pictures, and angrily told them he could do anything he was challenged to do. The kids soon began to treat him as a mental stranger, even though they admired his extraordinary strength.

One day a couple of them teased him. I saw him leap the fence and give chase. He caught one, lifted him up bodily, and flung him ten feet over a fence on to old Bailey's lawn. The kid didn't stir. I ran out. Johnny was white. He was muttering unintelligibly.

'Get home,' I told him. 'Go on, get home.'

There was trouble about that. The kid, Freddy Alexander, went to hospital with shock and a broken ankle, and the old lady and I had to pay part of the medical expenses.

Johnny was twelve when that happened. The following five years shaped him like a gorilla. He swelled out around the shoulders, dwindled leanly, and walked with a rhythmic plod, though he was tall. His face had broadened, his bottom lip hung loose, and his eyes alternated between fixity and shiftiness.

He was a giant among men, let alone kids of his age, and he was vain about it. His size and his strength were an obsession with him. His power and might were invincible, he thought, and the thought made him absolutely fearless.

He said to me: 'Billy, you get a gun and see if you can shoot Johnny.'

How could I argue with a delusion that made him believe

himself a superman? I told him it was impossible to get a gun.

'You get a gun, Billy' he repeated, as though he hadn't heard me; 'and shoot a bullet into Johnny, and Johnny won't die. You do that.'

'You don't have to prove it to me,' I said. 'I know.'

That satisfied him, but it didn't satisfy me. I talked to the old lady about it: 'Don't you think he ought to be seen to? He's going to end up in trouble if we don't do something.'

'I've thought, Billy; I don't know what to do. Still, he's not doing anyone any harm'.

'No one but himself,' I told her. 'He's King Kong. He's the strongest man in the world. He's invulnerable and immortal. One of these days someone is going to show him that his blood spills like anyone else's, and that he can die with the rest of us.'

'Don't talk like that,' she snapped. 'Don't say it.'

'Well, it's true. Unless he's gratifying his ego, unless someone is telling him what a Hercules he is, he isn't happy. He's got people frightened of him and he loves it. And, Ma, it's something he's not going to grow out of. Don't you think the people in this town talk about us? Queer, peculiar, is the kind of way of putting it. You ought to hear 'em down at the billiard room of a night. I'm getting to think he's not human myself!'

I saw her eyes, and I turned, to see Johnny lumber in. He was quiet. I knew he'd overheard me. I told Ma I was going down for a game of snooker and went out.

Johnny didn't say anything to me. He walked down the street with me next day. I saw the respect men gave him, while all the time knowing how they gigged him to each other. They'd all had him in for their amusement: lifting engines bodily out of cars at Liffey's garage, picking up sixteen-stone men, one hand, and holding them above his head, hoisting trucks up by their bumper bars to the height of his waist.

Suddenly, in the quiet of that street, there was a growing commotion from the other end like rain coming over a mountain, a haze of dust, and the thunder of hooves. Men and women were scattering into shops. The runaway horse was a frisky grey from McCarthy's stables. Its rearing head and wild eyes were visible though the dust, and the noise of its galloping was loud in my ears. I jumped back into a doorway, but Johnny ran out in front of it as if it were a windblown paper instead of a juggernaut of flesh and bone.

The horse pounded down in its terror, there was dust, and Johnny was clutching its neck, swinging along under it so that the animal's head was jerked down with its tossing burden. It stumbled in a red vapor of dust, struggling and whinnying on the earth while the man pinned it by the head. I ran up and others followed; and gradually the horse was soothed to its feet, flare-eyed and drip-mouthed, its shocked nerves calming.

Johnny was standing there, dusty and grinning, a crazy light of self-idolatry in his eyes. Everybody shook his hand and commended his bravery. As for me, I felt water-kneed. It was a wonder he wasn't killed.

That night I was playing billiards when he came in looking for praise. I began to feel a bit nervous, remembering that he had overhead my remarks to the old lady. Everybody nodded to him, and he nodded back. But it didn't come in the quantity he'd no doubt expected, and he looked disappointed. After watching the play for a little while, he came over to me and said: 'Billy, who says things about Johnny? What things, Billy?'

Everybody heard him and everybody was quiet. Maybe they expected something to happen, for Johnny had never been in the billiard room before. The brilliant pools of the arcs swept down on the green tables and the colored balls. Men moved as on slippers, idly chalking cues.

'What are you talking about?' I snarled at Johnny, for I knew what his mien signified. 'Why don't you go home and keep the old lady company? You know she likes you to be around at night.'

His face was a cold flat slab of rage: 'I catch anyone say anything about Johnny — you catch anyone you tell me, Billy, and I'll do this to him. I'll do this.'

He was standing at the middle of the table. He clutched it underneath and wrenched, and there was a crack and splinter of floorboards. He tipped the table over on its side, and the balls struck and rolled everywhere. A shout came ahead of Lanny McRae, the proprietor, as he rushed from down back.

Lanny was a big man and hot-tempered. He blasphemed, and the words shook out of him in passion: 'You crazy bastard: Who do you think you are? Why don't they put you away? By God — you'll pay for that table — you'll pay every penny or I'll land you behind bars for six months and in a padded cell for the rest of your life.'

Johnny fastened his hands around Lanny's throat, jerked him off the floor like a rag, swung him around and dashed him back against the wall. I yelled at the others to step in and get Lanny away, grabbed Johnny and hugged him while he dragged me with him.

Then the police came. I fell back, saw the batons rise, heard them crunch, saw Johnny reel, stunned; and the handcuffs clicked on his wrists. He didn't quieten for ten minutes. And they didn't bother trying to shift him till he did.

Lanny was talking, plaster-white, dabbing at this head with a handkerchief: 'Crazy as a coot, I tell you. He'd stand in front of a train and expect it to bounce back when it hit him. He would, so help me.'

Everybody laughed and snickered. The fury came up on Johnny's face. His lips quivered back in a snarl and he bounded to his feet, jerking his arms. The handcuffs snapped like string.

Frightened men fell back, panicking. The police rushed in with their batons raised. Johnny felled them with terrible downward blows of his bunched fists. Lanny McRae pelted through the door into the street and Johnny surged after him.

We made a rush to the door but there was no sight of them. The men were ugly. Some of them helped the policemen who, shaken and bruised, tore off to the station. In a few minutes four or five of us went after them. There were three constables there armed with rifles, and a sergeant who carried a revolver.

131

'God Almighty, you're not going to kill him?' I asked, horrified. 'Let me go out. I'll find him, and I'll bring him back here.'

The sergeant's face never broke its hard lines: 'Your brother's a danger,' he said. 'We'll only use the firearms if we have to.'

We all went out into the street. It was deserted. Shadows lay among the raggle-taggles of cold light and street signs swung and creaked in the wind. A group of men came toward us. Some of them had waddies. I looked hard at one, old Dan Hardman, and he said to me: 'I'm sorry, Billy, but we don't want him around here anymore. He's not safe. There's only one place for him.'

The police sergeant split up his men, and the citizens ranged themselves with each group. I went with the sergeant's bunch. We walked down Lambeth Street. In a lane we found McRae, twisted like a rag doll in the roadway, his neck broken. The sergeant sent a man for the ambulance, and we went on towards the next cross-street.

A man there in dressing gown, with slippers on his feet, asked what was wrong. He said he heard a shriek. He said he saw Johnny running out of the lane across to the railway reserve.

We went there quickly, walking through the paspalum and rye, under the solitary moaning pines: no lights save the stars and the green round-eyed signals. The moon began to rise, laying a sheen along the horizon; blackly objects stood against it. We passed the poison tanks, stopping every now and then for sound of the fugitive.

Suddenly one of the constables rapped out a whisper: 'Look! There he is!'

Atop the embankment, against the silver skyline, a hunched man was walking. The sergeant lifted his rifle. I grabbed it desperately: 'Sergeant, don't! Let me try first. He'll listen to me.'

The sergeant nodded, reluctantly, and I turned and walked

towards Johnny. He stopped dead when I called his name. I walked nearer. He was thirty yards away, a man-shape black as tar.

'Johnny,' I said. 'Come on home, boy. The old lady's worried about you.'

His voice sounded nothing like his own: 'Johnny is the strongest man in the world. There is nothing to beat Johnny. You go and tell Lanny McRae, Billy. You tell Lanny that.'

The sergeant and the others were up with me then. I could hear their controlled breathing.

'Johnny, I've got a gun here. If you don't come down and come quiet I'll have to kill you, Johnny.'

He shrieked: 'No, Billy, you can't kill Johnny.' He stood upright, gesturing, baring his chest as the target. 'You shoot that gun, Billy; you can't kill Johnny.'

We could hear her then in the distance; the thrumming air of her coming. I walked on, my palms cold wet with sweat, till I was fifteen yards from him and looking up.

His voice was crestfallen: 'Shoot, Billy. Why don't you shoot the gun, Billy?' Then an excited babble broke from his lips: 'Quick, Billy, you get Lanny! You tell Lanny to watch me. You get him and I'll show him, Billy.'

The sergeant was beside me: 'We'll just have to rush him, get him off those rails and overpower him. Come on.'

The train was louder, her coughing gride shaking up the sleeping echoes; the air racing with her portent; to the west a flash of light slid over the trees as she rounded Parkinson's Bend.

Johnny heard the rustle as we swarmed up the embankment. He yelled obscenities and pelted along the line. He was screaming: 'You tell Lanny, Billy. Johnny can stop a train. Johnny can. You see'

And he was running and stumbling, and we were after him; then the great Cyclopean disc of light was aiming straight towards us, swimming through space; there was ruby mist floating back over her tender, and flickering red sheets of air pulsing at her cabin sides; her throttle was open, she hammered and snorted.

And against her in the middle of the rails was Johnny, standing there upright, his elbows bent as he drummed on his chest; and I was sick with dread, and sobs clicking in my throat. I saw him as a mute, ignorant animal, like something out of prehistory, mentally sightless of the power of the monster ranged against him, oblivious of everything save the conviction of his own unconquerability.

And as we fell away to the sides, unable to do anything else, I snatched a rifle and aiming at the shaggy knob of his head haloed with horrible light, I pumped the bullets and saw him crash: and the engine was a black wall, and the train a screaming stream of sound and a red light trailing away into the darkness.

I did it for him. I tell him that. I tell myself. I couldn't see him cut to pieces alive, disappointment flying in the ruptured and scattered shreds of his being; but I hear his unforgiving voice, and see his grief-struck face, and the words are no less alive because they are the words of the dead. You killed Johnny before he had the chance to show you. You killed him, Billy.

WITHOUT YOU IN HEAVEN

*T*his was the woman I took for mate, and I wanted no other.

I met her in Tintinara, the daughter of a cocky there, and I married her and gave her seven children. They're all alive but the fourth, and the fourth was the one she loved most, if a mother can love one child more than another.

When I met her she was plump but sleek, the colour of an apricot, with hair like the mane of a brumby, golden red. Even three years with me changed all that. She was lean, the skin dark and tight on her face; but she was healthy and jolly still. She knew when she threw in her lot with me what to expect. She could have had an easy life. She had been city-educated. She was refined and gentle.

The world I took her into was a world of hard living: one for men, and if for women then women with tongues and wrists like men: working here, camping there, eating when you had something to eat. She knew all that, but she said: I'd rather be with you in hell than without you in heaven.

What I'm telling you might sound soft coming from a man, coming from me, but what I'm telling you is what I feel in here. It's what I feel. I don't tell it to anyone, not even her.

135

In that season of our wedding she came pea-picking with me out of Port Pirie, and the same year we picked grapes at Goodnight. When I got a shed just over the border in Victoria we lived in a tent, and she cooked for me, and sometimes came up on the board and swept for the picker-up. She was popular. The shearers took the hat around and bought her a present at the cut-out.

I was wood-cutting on the Murray when she had the first kid. She had it alone, and in six months it was punching holes in my chest like a Dempsey. No clean hospitals for that kid. Only a log cabin and a bag stretcher. But you wouldn't have known.

The three of us battled over to the east coast of Spencer Gulf, and I worked in the phosphate works at Wallaroo. And I made good money bag-sewing during the wheat and barley harvests.

The second kid was born at Marree. They wanted fettlers on the line there, and I had a cut at that. We were still at Marree when she had the third baby, and I could show nothing for the months of toil I had put in. Every penny seemed to go on tucker. There was nothing to save.

I had two jobs offered me, well-sinking, dam-scooping, working with camels. I'd done that before, during the Depression when I worked for rations. I was thinking about them when a feller going through to Alice told me about the opal fields north of Port Augusta; and how they were making fortunes there, and you were a pretty unlucky sort of bird if you couldn't make wages.

So there we went, she and I and the three kids, into that desolation — the earth looking as if it had been joggled by an earthquake and set back solid in red sandhills and gibber plateaus, shorn bleak, stunned with the heat, where the wind burned and glazed the air over the white kopi dumps, and the silence was just as if you were deaf.

We went out with the mailman over the rough road, and we had nothing when we arrived. But the little settlement of gougers rallied round. The storekeeper, who was also the boss of the field, told me he'd grubstake me till I struck opal. He gave me a large tent, too. Pay for it as you can, he said, but don't worry. There were only about forty people there, and he grubstaked most of them, and they settled their debts when they sold their parcels. They lived in dugouts torn under the hills, in tents, bag humpies, tin shacks.

I built a platform out of boxes, stuffed a tick with canegrass, and we were right for a bed. She sewed bags together and made waggas. I fixed up a table out of boxes, and used kerosene boxes for seats. We used a primus for cooking and an open fire. It was fine, and we were happy. The fellers lent me tools, one a pick, another a spade, others caps, detonators and jelly, augur and windlass.

I worked hard for three months, and I never saw a sight of colour though I went down shafts that had yielded fortunes and drove them further, and sank fresh shafts of my own. She loused the dumps, sifting the dirt that came up, and she found chips which she bottled and a few nobbies that the buyers bought for a quid or two.

Then I got on to the stuff, and it was rich — scarlet and bronze flashes, the best, and I thought, this is it. I dreamed of shoals of money, and us right for a while. But I had only taken a hundred and twenty pounds worth when the pocket petered out as unexpectedly as it had begun. Still, that was something, and it made us feel that our luck had changed. I was able to pay up a sixty pounds store bill and start off with a clean slate, buying goods until the money ran out. That was a good feeling.

The way she cooked and managed eased the bill in the next few months, when all I made was a living. She'd go out with a rifle and bring home a rabbit. She wore an old slouch hat and a pair of denims, and went barefoot around the house. We called it the house. The tent, I mean. At Christmas she organised a party for the kids on the field. About ten there were altogether. They had drinks and cake and carnival caps and a few toys from Adelaide; and it was something to see those kids bogging in and blowing tin whistles and trumpets, and banging drums. Away out in that country it was something.

Newchums came to the field, railwaymen putting in their holidays, and white-faced blokes from the cities, and some of them just buried a pick, so to speak, and took away three or four hundred quid. There were a couple of youths who came on a Saturday, went down an old abandoned shaft, cleaned the dirt out, blasted the drive and struck a rich pocket just a few feet from where the last man, defeated, had left off. They got six hundred quid's worth of the stuff and they were gone on the Thursday. That was the way of it: while some of us who had been living there eighteen months and more had scarcely made tucker.

I felt discouragement before she did, and was talking about moving off, but she didn't want to quit. I lay down on the bed thinking, tired in body and in spirit, tired of the struggle for a living. Maybe I should have followed in the old man's footsteps; taken advantage of the good education he had given me. Maybe . . .

'Come and scrub my back,' she said.

She was haunched down in the washing tub, having a bath. I took the nail brush and started scrubbing foam between her shoulder blades till the flesh came up pink.

'Well, what do you say?' I asked her.

'No, let's stay on a while longer,' she said. 'You never know — this time tomorrow we might be rich.'

'Tomorrow! Yeah!'

'Oh, don't be an old gloomy Gus. That's not like my bloke. You don't want to let a passing feeling get you down.'

I knew that was right: a passing feeling.

'Say we do go away,' she said. 'Where do we go? Won't it be the same, settled here for a while, there, and everywhere? Working, moving on? We've got a roof. We eat. We can't expect any more than that wherever we go, and so long as we stick here there's always the chance we'll better ourselves.'

I knew that was right, too.

'You don't think I'm complaining, do you?' She started to laugh in the silence. 'Well, do you?' She flipped the water from her hands in a spray on my face, laughing and saying: 'Sweet old blockhead.'

'That do?' I asked her.

'Do? You sure I've got some skin left?'

I lay down on the bed, folded my hands behind my head and looked at her. She stood up to dry herself, and she was lean and smooth as a wind-cut hill; her flesh was creamy, with drops of silver water on her brown shoulders and brown face. And, looking at her, I saw her through all that tiredness the way I'd seen her that first night of our honeymoon in that dingy pub room. She was fresh, and clean, and healthy.

'Gentlemen turn their faces,' she reproved.

'Come here.'

I touched her hair, ran my fingers through it, and it was dry and rough like a corn husk. I thought: You've starved, you've battled with me, and yet you can lie there, glowing like a cat on the hearth; your flesh is like silk rubber and sweet-smelling; your mouth is a soft bloom, and there is a long and lazy slant to your eyes, and you are ready for me: and I am a rough man with hard bones, in grubby clothes, smelling of sweat, dusty-haired and with a week's growth of beard: and this is out here in a desert wilderness, in a familiarity of ancient silence where the tongue of man is a primitive and alien trespasser; out here under a roof of canvas, on a bed of canegrass, with a floor of earth and the rude implements of our living about us; what man has more than I have at this moment?

The months went by. Men came and went. The Dorsett family moved on and left us their nanny goat. The kids got a lot of fun out of it, and the milk was a great change after the tinned kind. I kept plugging along, the storekeeper standing by me. I owed him seventy pounds when I had another good strike that brought me sixty pounds.

I went into his store cut into the hillside, raftered with pine, and pushed the lot across the short box counter towards him. He tore three dockets, black with items, from the back of my account book, crumpled them and threw them away. That was his style. He did it with all of us when we paid our bills. Sometimes it was one docket, sometimes two, depending on the size of the debt. Some said he could afford to do this because his prices were high, and he made it up with a sixpence here and a threepence there; he gave nothing away. For my part, it was a concession that came from his heart, because I thought him white all through.

She had her fourth kid, and the neighbours helped her with it. I looked at these women: they were stringy and lank with faces like leather, cracked with the wind and the sun and hard living, their eyes sewn into pouches, their hands big and strong. They could cut a sheep's throat, swing an axe, dig a grave. She would do these things, too, but whereas they looked the part she never did. But their hearts were in the right place.

The kid was a sickly little sprat from the start. There was a priest who visited the field every so often, and he christened it. She had her way and called it Bill, after her old man. He had died a month before. You wouldn't have known it, though; and they had been great pals.

When Bill was six months old we took him into Port Augusta, and the doctor said he would have to have special foods and medicines. Anything that was going that kid got — croup, measles, chickenpox, whooping cough. Then, after a year he seemed to pick up a bit. She never spared him. He came in for special handling, though not coddling, and she worried about him. It took a lot out of her, but she never complained. It was a good thing the other kids ate like rabbits and bullocked and banged through life. It lightened the job.

The kid was two years old when he got some fever. He just went down like that. All the week he was as spry as a grasshopper, and we were only saying how well he looked; then this thing hit him and he lay burning in a cot I had fashioned out of canvas and timber. I was behind in debt to the storekeeper again; about fifty pounds. And there wasn't any hope of working. The ground was sludge, red mud that put ten-inch stilts on your boots in a dozen yards. The rain had come with a wild lash, disappeared in a blaze of flame, and come again.

The road was impassable; the mail truck couldn't get through, and the store was running low.

She nursed that kid night and day, calm-faced, dogged. Then she said: 'We'll have to try and get him to hospital. I don't know what else to do.'

'We'll get him there then.'

'You're welcome to my bus,' Wally Hamilton said, 'if you think you can make it.'

Jim Pacey didn't think we could: 'She'll be up over the hubs before you get halfway across that flat. Another day with that sun on it and she might dry out enough.'

'Yes, and what if it rains again?' I asked.

'We've got to get him through,' she said. 'We can't wait.'

I had little hope, but I thought we could try; and when it was settled the news spread and people came.

'Don't worry about the other children, dear — we'll look after them.' That was Mrs. Adams.

Old Fred Crouse pulled a tobacco tin from his hip pocket: 'You'll need money in there,' he said. 'Fiver ought to help. I ain't gonna scream for the police if I don't get it back.'

Others pressed money into my hands. There was nothing I could say. Only feel. And I couldn't express that feeling.

Some of the women helped her throw a few things in a case. She wrapped up the kid and we got away.

It was four o'clock in the afternoon. I didn't use the road all the way, but made my own, skimming in a wide arc the bogs and waterholes. At five the clouds shaped up, inked in the sky and hung threatening. Five times I tried to get through the red flour of the sandhills, and made it when our hopes were giving out.

The dark came quickly. A sleet of rain smashed against the windscreen. I took the truck off the road, across country, tea-tree slapping at the sides. The rain went off.

'How is he?'

'Just like a fire,' she said. Her voice was quiet, controlled. 'You're doing well.'

She touched my arm, squeezed it.

We kept going for an hour, slipping, sliding, slithering, bouncing, bucking, but going. I'd taken my coat off to wrap around the kid, protecting him from the wet gusts. There were no side curtains. The spray showered back. When the ute stalled in that darkness, shuddering, the rear wheels slathering around uselessly, I gave her all she'd take. But it was no good.

I left the engine running and jumped out. The wheels were churning in the thick ooze, but sinking deeper. I cut the engine. The wheels blobbed down, the mud sucked and buried them to the hub caps. There were no tools in the truck. I got down and started to scoop the stuff away with my hands, piling it back like the thick silt of a dam bottom. In a minute she was out of the truck, helping, down on her knees raking the other wheel free.

I started the truck up while she stood behind thrusting her weight against it. The wheels hummed, slapped, the truck lifted, jerked back, lifted, jerked back.

'Stay there,' she called. I looked back. She ripped off her coat, tore it in two down the seam, and thrust the cloth in each hole against the wheels. The wheels gripped, lifted, and she came running round, grabbed up the blanketed child and laid him on her lap. I could hear her harsh breathing.

I kept that jalopy going and feared to talk, expecting the trouble again, hanging on to my breath.

We cut through Pimba, and across the gibber plain, and God was with us from then on. We struck Port Augusta at noon next

142

day and got the kid to hospital. They didn't hold out much hope, but they'd work, they said.

She didn't want to leave the hospital, but I told her we'd get a pub room and a clean-up and something inside us, and come back. My clothes were stiff with mud. It was dried in blobs on her face, in her hair, plastered against her dress. I got her away.

She stayed at the hospital all that night, quiet, calm, and I sat with her. In the morning we went down the street and into a cafe for breakfast. The Greek was just putting the chairs down off the tables and swabbing out. He made up eggs and bacon.

'You must be dog tired,' I told her.

'No,' she said. 'I'm all right.'

'If you went back to the pub and had a couple of hours sleep you'd feel better.'

'No, I'll be all right.'

I felt ashamed then, because I needed sleep, and I wanted the excuse of her sleeping to take it.

She couldn't eat all her breakfast. She wasn't cheerless; no. She kept talking to me and smiling, and saying when Billy got well we might go and live in Adelaide for a while; and perhaps a city job would suit me for a few months. But she had a keyed-up tension about her.

We went back to the hospital, and they told us the kid was showing signs of improvement, but it was too early yet to be sure. The day dragged away. I went for a walk, wandered down Commercial Road to the railway wharf and watched them unloading coal from a Newcastle collier. I had a beer with the flies and went back to the hospital. There was nothing new.

At nightfall I persuaded her with the help of the doctor to come back to the hotel and have some rest. We had tea, and went up to the room with the four-poster bed and the naked, fly-specked globe. I felt like lead and lay down. She sat down beside me.

'Have some sleep or you'll drop.' I couldn't help the anger in my voice.

'No. I'm all right. You have some, darling.'

143

I fought to keep my eyes open. I fought. I was talking to her, hearing myself, and then not hearing. And suddenly I opened my eyes and the drowsiness fell from me. There was a dead silence, a blowfly buzzing somewhere in the room, the blind tapping gently against the open window. The light was on. I turned in the bed. She was sitting in a chair looking at me. She had her hat on. Her face was very white.

'Where are you going? What's the time?'

'Nearly dawn.'

'Can't we wait till morning to go to the hospital?'

'He's dead,' she said.

It got into me then. She hadn't slept. She'd been to the hospital. And I'd been sleeping. Christ, I thought, a man's weak.

'They did their best,' she said. And I understood.

A man grows his grapes and they hang full on the vines; the hail strikes and a year of toil is lost in the ruinous hour; but the man braces up his heavy heart and hopes for a better year next time: the drought hollows the bellies of sheep and they die in the hatred of the sun; but the grower knows this is a mood of the country, and he knows there will be a green year. And what weapons do they take against the bushfire that burns them out of a home they got together through toil and sweat and poverty and grind, and toasts their land, bloating the one cow and the one horse, and bringing their world to ashes? They live, and go on living through a thousand griefs and failures, though they are dazed and heartsick at the time.

This child of ours was dead, and that was like the bushfire and the hail and the drought.

But she was calm still. Whatever she was feeling she was keeping it cooped up there inside her. But I didn't realise it all then. I jumped out of bed and lit a cigarette and told her she had to have some sleep. She said she was all right. But she didn't resist when I took off her hat and led her to the bed.

'Yes, I'll rest now,' she whispered.

When she was lying down, her eyes glazed with fatigue, she smiled slightly at me, and said: 'You're good to me.'

The funeral was over, and she was absolutely calm, and we decided to go back that evening. She said she had promised to take the kids back something, and she went and bought some lollies and a few comics. We didn't get away till about nine, and we stopped to eat sandwiches and boil the billy about dawn. It was cloudy and you could smell the rain. We didn't waste any time lagging; we had to race it.

The mud was still caked on the steering wheel, and came off in powder against my hands. We stopped at the spot where we had been bogged and she picked up the torn coat hard with embedded clay, black with mud.

'I'll wash it and mend it, and it'll do me a few turns yet,' she said.

I listened for the memory in her tones, but there was none.

'One of these days I'll get you such a coat you won't believe it's you wearing it.'

'You will too,' she smiled.

We were running into the storm: masses of bruised cloud fomenting and boiling, with a sharp wind galloping before it. We got over the sandhills and across the flat when it came like a cloudburst. Like a cyclone out of Broome. I gave that truck everything. Between sky and earth was a thick, ashen roaring wall, with wild twisting trees as in a mirage, and smashing in a white surf against the windscreen. Through the curtainless side-windows it drove in like a shot of pebbles, blinding me, so that she put her arm across my back and shielded my eyes with a hand held like a blinker.

The rain thundered and crashed its way about us so that we were sogged like sponges. The road came up now and then, a deluge of mad water; the wheels rolled. Over the hill we saw the murky phantom of the settlement, and it came nearer. Then she clutched my arm with a sharp spasm of dismay: 'The house! It's gone!'

The slope was bare where our tent had stood, and the skyline was unfamiliar. What had we been doing talking about getting home, hurrying home, God, to be home; to get dry and shelter? And there it was, all of it hurled down and torn, slashing on the beaten earth, flooded out, everything, water running, bouncing, roaring, like rust and mustard, filling up the pits our boots made.

We stood there staring while it streamed off us; and then I pulled a flap of the tent up and fixed it on to the truck, and she got a sapling, rammed in the earth, and hitched another end to that, so that we had shelter of a kind. We pushed in under it against the drumming canvas, and there was the kids' goat, shivering, morbid, half-drowned on the bed. Furious, I grabbed its ears, hurled it off and kicked at it fiercely and half chased it out into the torrent. And I felt relieved. I felt better.

Turning back, I saw her sitting on the end of the bed, looking at the kid's clothes, Billy's clothes, tumbled out of the overturned port, limp and muddy, and a grubby, one-eyed teddy bear that was his; and the sight of them must have been too much for her; she was crying terribly, with an ugly face, shrunken and small as if there were no bones left firm in her body.

BEYOND THE BELL

*T*hat's what they thought, anyway. They picked him up and put him in. A woman came along there five hours later, white-faced and without her hat: and the sergeant brought him out, took her bail money, and said: 'He's all yours, missus.'

He watched the woman take the man's arm and lead him gently away. 'Frankie, didn't you tell them?' she protested tenderly as they walked along the street.

He shook his head.

'Why not?'

He didn't answer. He muttered something thickly, but it wasn't an answer.

'You should have, Frankie.'

He shot the words suddenly, jibingly: 'You think they'd believe me?'

'Didn't they know you, though?' she persisted. 'Who you were?'

'I don't know, I don't know,' he said, irritably, wearily. 'What difference does it make?'

She told him softly, quickly, that it was all right. But the unfairness of it hurt her. He was no drunk. Whatever else he was, he was not that.

She wondered what he'd been doing. Nothing — nothing more than stumbling along maybe, with that gait he couldn't help. Or sitting on the kerb with his head in his hands, like the last time she found him: lost in the jungle of his thoughts, and the thoughts breaking in tortured sound from his lips, loud and fierce, and himself unaware of it.

'Where are we going now?' he said.

'Home.'

'Home!' He spat the word bitterly.

'You must be hungry.' She hurried out the words. 'I've got a nice tea for you, and there's some of that favorite . . .'

'Home for the loony. There he goes up the stairs, wobble-nut. There he is, singing out again in his sleep. Watch him. Look out for him. He's not all there.'

She gripped his arm: 'Ah, Frankie, don't — it's not right.'

'Follows him everywhere, she does. Eyes open twenty-four hours a day — that's her.'

'Frankie, please. Please, Frankie.'

Ears listening. Heads sticking out the door. Talking to one another. The gossip that goes with the sale of carrots at the fruiterers, the topic at the pub, news to wash down with the supper at night: a headline in the lives of those rats in their holes at the residential. That's what he'd said a hundred times. That's what he was thinking now.

She held his arm tightly, looking up at his worn face as they passed into the light. Thirty years of age carrying a face of forty, as though someone had fitted him with a mask.

Back home there was a picture of him on the mantelpiece: one she was always looking at. Showing him, just the throat and head from the high turtleneck of the sweater to the blond, shaggy hair, and a great grin in between. This wasn't the man in the picture.

'I'd swap them any day — God, how I wish I could.'

'What?' he said.

'Nothing, Frankie.'

'Thinking loud again.'

148

'I'm sorry.'

The fog was coming down early, breathing out of the darkness like a wet, cold smoke, blearily ringing the lights. The footpath glistened and echoed their footfalls. A match flared in a doorway, picking out the contour map of a face, and died behind the ruby dot of a cigarette.

A man swung up in front of them, and cried gaily: 'Ah, see you found him all right, Grace. Where I said?'

'Yes.'

'I thought it was Frankie I saw. How are you, son?'

'Never better, Joe,' Frankie said grimly.

'That's the stuff. Say, Grace, I'd like to walk along with you, but I've got a meet on in a few minutes.'

'That's all right, thanks Joe,' she said.

'I'll pop around Sunday night for a yarn, if that's okay. You be in, Frankie?'

Frankie nodded: 'Be glad to see you, Joe.'

They went on, and Joe looked after them, and his smiling face was closed up. He kept looking after them, hearing them even out of earshot. He knew Grace ten years ago when she was eighteen. He'd introduced Frankie to her. Matchmaker Joe, Cupid McCurdy, he reflected wryly. God, why in hell did it have to be him — making it tough for her, making it tough for Frankie, because he hated himself for what he was to Grace.

'He said Sunday night he'd be around,' Frankie pointed out.

'That's right, dear.'

'I won't be home Sunday night,' Frankie said. 'I don't want any talk. He always starts dragging it up.'

'It's only because he thinks you like to talk about it,' she soothed him.

'Well, I don't!'

'No.'

'I don't like it, see?'

'Well, he won't come, Frankie. He never does, does he? Not lately.'

She knew Joe understood.

They turned, and walked on in silence down the narrow, dim street. The lights were only a hole here and there in the blackness. Fences leaned out like snaggled teeth. There was a shop on a corner, glowing like a beacon: a mixed business, poky, crammed with goods: run by a gab of a woman with a pile of dyed, yellowish-grey hair and a pencil stuck in it.

Grace veered slightly, piloting Frankie towards it. She felt the resistance jolt in his arm.

'I want to get milk for the baby, dear,' she explained.

'I'm not going in there.' He stopped and pulled away from her.

She looked anxiously at him: 'It won't take a minute.'

'I'll wait.'

She hesitated, unsure whether or not to leave him. Then she saw he sensed her mistrust, and she smiled. 'All right,' she said lightly, but the look of anxiety came back on her face when she turned into the shop.

There were three people there. Grace would have to wait her turn. Frankie drifted on a little way down the street. He stood teetering on the kerb looking across the road. The row of tenements stared back, their windows blind and grey as oysters.

A lout in a tight coat, a cocky hat, and swinging jaunty shoulders approached with a squib of a mate.

The lout tapped Frankie on the shoulder: 'Well, if it ain't the champ. How's tricks?'

'I don't know you,' Frankie said.

'Sure you do. Me and you used to be sparring partners, remember? You was a tiger for showing me things, remember? Say, who's the jerk behind you?'

Frankie turned his head, and the lout hit him solidly behind the ear. Frankie stumbled. He faced up, wobbling, his hands jerking mechanically.

'Show us how you can stop this one, champ.'

A blow landed between his eyes.

The lout laughed, his eyes bright, and picked off the helpless man. 'And this one,' he rapped, uppercutting Frankie. Frankie fell and rolled over on his side, moaning slightly.

The lout stood there, talking big, and his scrawny mate gaped in admiration. They started running only when Frankie's wife came from the shop, saw him lying there and cried out. Two others came pelting from the shop, and a woman from across the road hurried up.

Grace put her hand under Frankie's head, cushioning it. The blood was seeping through the battered flesh under his eyes as through sponge rubber. There was a dead dullness in his eyes, nothing else.

None of the bystanders moved. The woman who ran the shop said to another in a hoarse whisper: 'Them hooligans — great caper they're on to now, ain't it? Knocking him down just so they can skite they beat the ex-champion. Rotten curs — somebody ought to take to 'em with a whip.'

They helped Frankie to get up when they saw Grace helping him. Frankie shook himself away, staggered against the fence, hung on, head down, groggy.

Grace stood near him, unable to say anything, waiting. She touched his arm. His head jerked up suddenly, wildly, and he cried: 'What are you doing, you fool. Get away!'

Her hand only tightened on his arm. They were silent, those looking.

'Look at you,' Frankie said. 'Look at you, like a dog with me. Don't you see what I am? Get away. Walk off now and don't come back. Go while the going's good.'

'Don't talk like that, Frankie.' The pressure tightened on his arm. 'Come on.'

He was saying something, choking on the words. She led him away.

The street was deserted except for them: and she could see it filled with them that used to fill his life — the faces like beads on a string, the babel of voices; those that lived by him and on him and with him: from gyms, newspapers, stadiums, training camps, promoters' offices, tout joints, all criss-crossing like searchlights in the sky, pinpointing him.

Going up with him to the bright, brief glory of the championship, but dropping away as he fell. Not falling with him, but dropping away and leaving him, the exploited to pay for the exploitation, leaving his life cold and empty — like this street.

Frankie was crying with a subdued harshness. She held his arm, and stared haggardly at the darkness ahead. There was nothing else she could do.

THE FEUD

A man called Fingal lived with his family in a house in the shade of a great tree. The tree and Fingal were enemies. Every time he came out of the small paddock, where his potato bags stood, or a broken swath was in his corn — or when he came from the bush, with his shirt open and the axe on his shoulder — he saw the tree, and he sneered.

He could see it a mile off, from a peaky hillock, and when he came down along the windbreak, with the skiey backdrop behind it, in red and russet. It was a thick, massy monster, a hundred feet high, and wide as the shadow of a mountain. With the evening dying out in quiet colors, it went sable and ominous. There was a menacing witchery about it, as it towered over his little house.

And there was never a good air about it, but always evil, a cunning, waiting, patient evil. In the moonlight it was like a black cloud suspended by his dwelling, threatening to float into it and engulf it. When the dusk was well down, the light yellowing from the window gave no cheer, because he could see the horrible, stifling giant, standing without a movement. And in the morning, when the sun expanded through the trees in filtering radii, creating a golden haze like sunlight in western dust, that tree was evil, and no sun crept into its dark bosom.

When the storm came with a helter-skelter flurry, it unlimbered itself with a dreadful patience, like a calm but terrible man rolling up his sleeves. It threshed and creaked, growing more powerful, howling and soughing in thunderous fury; all the other trees were as sighing echoes of it.

It swung hard with a semi-gyration. It labored terrifically. And then, when the storm was gone — after its typhooning, after its invigorating bath and gymnastics — it moved gently, tired and exhilarated. To Fingal it looked more terrible.

His face, cracked like a walnut, came to glower naturally, and he even thought of the tree before he saw it. Its appalling personality gave him no rest. His senses gripped it and roiled it in the hate of his mind. One day, when he and his son were husking corn, the boy asked:

'When are we going to cut down the tree, Dad?'

'Soon.'

'You've been going to cut it down for a long time.'

'Yes. But it is a big job. I will destroy it soon.'

'Mum doesn't like you putting it off. She said she thought you was afraid of it, too.'

'Ah, your mother's a foolish woman,' he snapped. 'Afraid? That's likely. Me — afraid of a tree?' he scoffed. 'It's her that's put the fear of it into you all. She sets a fine example with her ideas. She's only trying to work up excuses to get away to the city. I know how she hankers after the grimy dump.'

The boy was about to remark again, but the father told him sharply to get on with his work. His wife was always nagging. If it wasn't one thing it was another. He resented her quality of determination that jarred with her spirit of submissiveness. She accused him of putting matters off: she detested the skimping and scraping that made management a travail.

She often came into Fingal's mind; the pale mouth working in the pale face, set into a frame of wispy hair. Always there was an exhausted air about her, as though she had walked a long, long way against a heavy wind. But he never pitied her, never sympathised with her. He just appreciated her as a utility that put a steaming meal before him. He would sooner watch ants steering down pencil tracks, and hate the tree.

He realised his inconsistencies, and he blamed the tree. He blamed it with a hatred that violated sense and reason. It had sucked out of him the very energy that had once made him industrious, and had left only indecisive remnants. And these remnants merely gave him, when necessity impelled, the spurts that caused him to plant corn, and sow potatoes and garden vegetables — enough to keep alive.

Two years ago he had come into the bush to make money and buy himself a farm. He had stood in the sun and seen the land, the wilding grass, bent and silver under the tameless wind, the trees straggling, and the great monster that drank their sappy blood. But then, at that time, he had not realized.

He had hewn the timber and built a house by the great tree, and, achievement filling his heart, had set out to clear the earth and make it arable.

Then, he saw the broken stumps all about the monster, and the withered grass, monuments to the gorging appetite of the brute; dumb witnesses to the thriving strength and power, the lushness and greenness for which they had died. And out farther it was reaching, with a vampiric lust, to other trees. The mark of death showed in their drying leaves, and their stripping bark and stunted growth.

Long ago it had sprouted up through the earth with others. They had all fought to live. They basked in the sun, they breathed in the air; the wind strengthened them, the frosts made them hardy. But not all.

This one, this rapacious giant, took much of what belonged to the others. It fought them. It dug its holt deeper, spread its roots and multiplied them, and clawed into the earth with a callous tenacity.

It grew, full of might that terrified the others. They struggled madly to reach up to the sun; the earth groaned with their straining. And then it weakened them. Slowly, with a horrible sureness, it drained away their life. They suffocated. It spread over them, a darkening enlarging shadow. Its sinewy legs bulged out of the earth, and gnarled themselves together. And the others died. For long years, this selfish murderer had killed to feed itself, encroaching on space even, and claiming an enormous gap.

Fingal cleared away the stumps. He cleared away the other trees: and always it howled in self-mourning. It ranted and dirged. It would grow no more. It could thieve no more. Then it was quiet, like a man done wrong, who schemes vengeance.

Fingal's crops were poor. He made little. He took an axe and gashed and severed its great toes. He ringbarked it, and waited, smiling grimly.

The tree apparently never noticed this disfigurement. It went on in awful, relentless calm. Fingal cursed. There was domestic trouble. His mind changed until he came near to psychosis.

He cleaned all the silt and leaves out of the guttering. The tank was choked up and the water polluted. Water had to be drawn from the creek until he had cleaned the tank. His wife complained. The garden was always sombre; only wilting things grew. The roots of the tree burst up under the house, and moved it slightly on its foundations.

And in his bed at night Fingal heard the sonorous sound of the tree. He heard in it a repining satisfaction, and a horrible gloating. He thought of ruin. He thought of his schemes gone astray: the trouble and the worry.

Well, he was not finished with it yet. He had done a lot to it; things that nothing else had done. Ferociously and tenaciously though it had killed and eaten, it could not domineer him. It could not break him. It could not oust his little house from its monarchal domain. But the tree was not done with him.

When he came in home that evening from the corn field, thinking of supper, his wife, on edge, told him straight she was sick of everything and was going away. He knew she was not fooling or bluffing.

'Where will you go?'

'I'll get work in the city,' she said. 'There's plenty of it. They're calling out for factory workers.'

He was thinking who'd look after him; who'd cook his meals.

'And what's more, Jimmy will get a job . . . a decent job,' she went on, determined. 'If you had any sense you'd come, too. Do you good to get into a different job, anyway.'

Fingal protested and persuaded, but there was no stopping her. The next day she left, the boy and the three-year-old baby with her. She had stood enough of that loneliness, and struggling and semi-starvation.

After that Fingal did nothing. He let his beard grow. He ate anytime and anything. The house was eerie, even in the daytime. At night it was full of creaks and winds. The bed was cold. He missed his children.

In an agony of hatred he cursed and swore at the tree. Always it was there, leaning over him in that goblin dwelling, sinister at night, glaring at him when he got out in the morning. His eyes squinted his hatred. His mouth showed bitter abomination, his clenched fists violence, his whole demeanour an aching revenge. He would kill it. He would chop it down if it took him years. He would spend every penny he had and dynamite it to bits. He would wipe the foul thing away for ever.

That night he was wakened into consciousness of the storm. He lay listening. He saw a blue flood of lightning, again and again. And he heard before the crash of thunder, a sizzling crackle and a terrible creak.

Quickly, he ran outside. In the flashes of lightning he saw the tree riven in two. He shouted with relief of affrighted surprise, with joy, with triumph; his enemy at last destroyed. Then his eyes stretched. The tree trembled, toppled, and fell crashing across the house, smashing it flat.

When they found Fingal his glazed eyes were still turned in terror, in numb fear and despair.

DADDA JUMPED OVER TWO ELEPHANTS

*T*wo years were left to him, and he lived with us, and he was happy. I am glad of that.

And when he died, they did in truth build the coffin extra wide to take his shoulders, and yet short, for there was nothing to him up and down. There is pride in that. Aloe and I were the only mourners, and when it was over I left her and went into town, and had a drink alone, seeing myself back there looking down at him, silent in wood, perished from time, and thinking:

This was my father, a good man that couldn't get the twist out of his character, and that twist put there back many a day; a chunky man with a heavy walk, yet quicksilver on his feet when it was to his purpose; scrubby hair, always damp with sweat; ridges on his forehead and fine markings under his eyes like scratches on the glass counters of lolly shops where children go.

He wasn't an old man, not really, though you'd swear he was to look at him and to listen to him — always talking of the good old days, and them ended for him not fourteen years ago. Before that he lived in the way that he liked to live.

That night in July: him sitting at that bit of a table with a

159

bottle, and bottles on the floor, dead marines, and talking to himself: Where is Queenie of the tightrope, and Marcus the strongman, and the lionman Rossetti, and Little Tich — where is he now, that king of them all? I remember and I remember and God bless them all: a fine company.

Going on like that about them, not even a weather-stained memory flapping on a backcountry hoarding. And the rain coming down in Palmer Street, falling in broken strings, falling in front of the window, jewelled as it passed the light; the slish of wet tyres, and the rumpty-tump from a harlot's house across the way.

And I'm on the bunk in the corner, watching the rain, hearing him, sometimes the words, always the sound.

'Two elephants, I did, so help me! Am I right, boy? Am I right?'

'Sure.'

He stared sourly, his lips pinched together in a scowl; 'What's the dirt in your voice for? What's bitin' you?'

'You've had enough of that stuff, dadda. What about turning in?'

'You don't seem to think it much that a man jumped over two elephants,' he challenged.

I rolled off the bunk and walked to the window, sick, angry, frustrated. Every anniversary of my mother's death the same: drunk and maudlin for a month. Week-end benders all the year round, but the big ritual every anniversary, and really a picnic over the last three years; as though with him the losing of the years made everything appear all the more hopeless. Your heart can stand it, maybe, but it wears an edge on your nerves.

'Do you?' he snapped. 'Turn around and face me like a man!'

'I'm facing you.'

'Well, do you?'

'Don't pick me, dadda.'

'I jumped over two elephants, I said, damn you!' he thundered.

'Yeah!' I flashed on him, the words gorging up. 'And you've

been jumping over elephants ever since. You flop in this, you jib at that. What's it matter? You jumped over two elephants, didn't you? That makes up for everything. But think it out. What's it worth? Who gives a damn? Some men can say: I gave him a feed when he was starving; she had a kid when she knew it meant the end of her life. That's what you call value. But you — you jumped over two bloody hulking elephants. That makes you a god, squares off your conscience, and patches every hole in your ego!'

Living on that phrase like a boxer, a jockey, an actor, the link with his days of greatness, the laurel wreath of idiom, the wonder boy of his time stuff. It was right what I said. But I wasn't belittling his feat. It was good. Great. Let it be. Take it out and talk about it now and again if you want to, but don't make a sermon out of it for breakfast, dinner and tea.

The rage went down in me and I was sorry for the words, and I kept looking at him, the artery in his right temple that swelled like a blue-red pipe under the skin when he hit the booze. He looked away unseeingly, and he spoke quietly: 'That's the truth of it, I 'spose. Well, what of it? Who asked you to stick it? If you had any brains in that big lemon you'd wipe me. You'd get away. Or is it guts you lack?'

'Get into your bed, dadda.'

'And make your own way. If your wasn't the big soft yob you are, you'd be gone long ago.'

'All right. All right. Come on, get on your pins, you're all in.'

I tried to help him up, but he wouldn't budge. He kept on swearing that he didn't want me clinging to him because he was no good for me, and crying fiercely to mean it. I'd heard it all before, so often before. All that and his remorse for his defeats and lapses; his repentance while he sinned, so to speak. And he did mean it. Maybe he was a millstone around my neck, but I never let him think that. We'd stick together, I told him. There was nothing I wanted to do that made his being with me an obstacle to doing it.

I got him on to the bunk, pulled off his boots and covered

him. He shut his eyes, and his lips moved with a fumbling weariness: 'You're a good boy, Jim; too good for the likes of me to be your father.'

He was asleep before I switched off the light.

I don't think he was a weakling. I think he was strong. He struck a crisis, and the crisis put a kink in his character; just as a cut tendon makes a man lame without destroying his leg. I can think of the tortures that beat up the human spirit, and physical wounds are nothing to them; the war that goes on deep inside a man and nobody knowing anything of its agony: and for that reason nobody is able to say rightly how weak a man is, though they will say it.

He suffered, and he suffered more because he fought suffering; and what I resented were the odds that brought him down in the fight to where he was — streaking him with a little of the waster, and a little of the bludger, and a little of this and that one among the types of common iniquity.

Clawing at wood that tore my fingers red, screaming at their screams, fighting the ones that dragged us away, until there were no screams, I remember, only flames and embers and ashes in turn. And them like toasted birds, as a man said.

I suffered, too, and I am sick still when I think of it; but it didn't change me the way it changed him. How could it? The relationship was different. She was my mother, but she was his wife, the fountainhead of his being; crystallised in her were all the objects of his existence, and while she fed it the current of his life flowed full.

Dadda was gone when I woke in the morning. His overcoat and suitcase, too. And I knew then he had walked out on me. There was no note like the last time. I lit the gas ring, made a cup of tea, and wondered what I'd do. I must have slept like the dead not to have heard him. My mind went back to the last time, and the note:

'Make this goodbye, Jim. You won't pull out, so I'm leaving you. I'll drop you a line sometime. Dadda.' Two years ago.

I thought for days about that. Then I had a hunch, helped out by talk he had made, and I went through the old circus towns, and I found him drinking in a pub at Warialda, and I brought him back.

Maybe that's what he's done again, I thought. I waited a couple of days to see if he'd turn up; then I decided to go after him. I went first to my Uncle Siddy, in his room of darkness, reading a Braille novel: groping my way to his bedside, for the landlady had taken away the bulb long ago. I asked him about dadda, and he boomed with a laugh: 'That old dipso still kicking? They don't make the firewater that can kill him, eh?'

'I've got an idea where he went, but I thought he might have told you. Did he come here?'

'Let him go, Jim. He wants it that way. That's the man your father is. He never stood in the road of any man; and least of all he'd stand in the way of his own flesh and blood. He'll drag you down. You'll never lift him up. And he knows it. He knows the man he was and the man he is, but he can't resist being the man he is. And he hates his guts for it.'

'All I know is, I can't let him go to the pack like that. Will you tell me — did he come here?'

'I'm not saying, Jim, but I'll tell you this: I don't owe him that fiver any longer. And that idea you've got — you follow it, Jim.'

I left that man to his double darkness, his listening fingers, and blundered to the door. He called after me: 'Like I told you before, Jim: remember your mother's not dead for him. It's like she's lost, and he just can't find her, that's all.'

It's funny how when you get in a train your memory's jogged, and you can think of all the times you travelled in trains in the past. Maybe it's the solitude. I was remembering myself in my mother's lap, warm against her warm breast, cradled in safety; and swaying and lurching in my father's arms down to the *gents*; and the night the dark man with the yellow tie was making eyes at my mother, and my father pulled his nose and jammed his hard hitter over his eyes; and my mother called dadda a jealous horror, but was proud of him all the same.

And the other times when we travelled in the caravan,

nosing through the darkness, the roads melting into light and rushing away under the wheels to darkness again; through towns huddled in sleep, and the smell of lions in the air. And that little caravan window I used to stare at and stare myself to sleep: on the roads in the high places like a breakwind of stars, it was; and I could see the wash of the wind against it. And then it came into my mind, the waifs and strays of their conversation that I overheard in the darkness on the blurry borders of sleep:

Oooh'd you feel the baby kick then?

No. Did he?

Here, put your hand on my tummy. There. Feel it?

Migord! It's a circus mule. Influence, that's what it is.

I don't think you really care at all about us having another one.

Not much: I'm tickled pink. I reckon I have bonza kids.

Who said it was yours, fathead?

Eh? he said, and then laughed. And she laughed, too.

And the memory of talk came fast, like a playback in my mind: the story of their meeting that I knew so well with him overing it that I might have been there when it happened. This woman out in the seats, and the smell of sawdust and orange peel, and a wind rolling the breathing roof of the canvas, the ring full of clowns and tumblers: balloon pants, criss-crossed eyes, crescent mouths:

You didn't know it then, but that was your mother golloping peanuts in the front row. Pretty as a doll, and the cutest buster cut I ever saw. One peep, and I said there's the chicken for my dinner. And soon as I appeared in the ring she squizzed me and fell like a Town Hall.

Like smoke, I did! I thought: What a show-off. Lord Muck, he was.

That's all right about you my girl. Well, there I am, boy, calling on folk from the audience to have a crack at Bessie, the rosinback; and there's a quid for the one who can stay three minutes. Just to show how easy it is, I demonstrate: bareback riding of the clowning kind, that's all.

And what a skite! You should have seen him. I was no fool on a horse, and I thought: I'll show you, Mister Big-head.

Yeah, believe it or not, she jumps up and hops into the ring. Full of brass. A picture to look at: in a dress with red and white stripes like a parasol, and a white hat the dead ringer for a mixing bowl. She'll ride that horse, says she, and saying it like I've been doing her wrong all her life. Okay, Sugar, I tell her; it's your neck you're breaking.

We'll see about that, smarty.

Off comes her hat, and her hair's so black you could take it for midnight. Off comes her buckled, high-heeled patent leather shoes that you could see your face in; and she pitches the lot into the lap of your Uncle Siddy, sitting in the front row with a grin to swallow a cat; not blind then, for the sod that threw pepper in his eyes came a long time after.

Well, in a couple of ticks the safety harness is fixed in place and she's up there, standing on Bessie's bare back as Bessie jogs around the ring. And, crikey, she's all right! And so are those long legs she's got!

You would be on to them!

Too right, but I didn't roar like the rest of the sheiks, you must admit. Flesh-pink stockings she wore, son, and sky-blue satin garters. Elegant, I tell you. But the seconds were ticking over, and she doesn't look like having a buster: so, thinking I'll have a bit of fun, I give the rope a pull and haul her off; and she swings through space, kicking her legs and squealing; and the crowd goes wild with laughter, and the boys all shouted more. And no wonder. For underneath all that flaming youth she was wearing pink flannelette bloomers.

Oh, I could have cried with humiliation.

I grinned, too, but I thought: How sensible, how very sensible. And as she swung around, fuming, and kicking at me, I said: Want me to teach you to ride, sweetie?

Ooo, you just wait, you aleck! Let me down! Let me down! Do it for nix, I will.

You painted ape, I'll smarther you!

So I hauled and up in the air she went again: and I held her there, and told the crowd what an entertainer, what a great little sport she was, and every bit worth the quid and another quid chucked in. And they clapped and yelled and whistled; and I let her down, and her eyes were full, and, God, I was sorry then. I had gone too far. But she wasn't finished. She made a swipe and I let it catch me under the chops and send me for a couple of back somersaults, to make her feel better. Then I anticked over to her, and, boy, did she kick, right and left, left and right, all over the legs and finally, as I turned, fair in the backside.

Of course the audience went hysterical with laughter, and that was the greatest night we had for a long time. Well, it wasn't hard after that. I nosed her out and made my apologies. That Uncle Siddy was a good scout. He was in there ramming for me, and before you could say: dip me hat, I was knocking her into a real classy bareback rider; and, to give you an idea of the speed, we were married inside three weeks, before the circus left that town.

That right, Mum?

My mother laughed: Siddy might have been ramming for you, but what you didn't know, my lad, was that he was helping me to hook you. You were a goner from the start, but you didn't know it.

And they both laughed, happy as angels about it.

There it was, myself thinking of my mother and father all the way in the train till it stopped at Moree. I found no trace of him in the town, and I went on to Warialda, and a publican when I asked him remembered: A little joker with big shoulders and some gab about jumping over two elephants. Yeah, he was here, 'bout three days ago. The johns pinched him.

At the police station they told me dadda, locked up for drunkenness, had bailed himself out, and they hadn't seen him since.

I took the train to Inverell. It's a pretty sizeable town. But I was lucky. I struck a barman, and he knew dadda, and he said:

'His boy! Hell — you mean that dark-headed, nuggety kid I used to see him with? Well, strike me dead, don't time fly? I wouldn't have known you.'

And he was a talky type, and he went on magging: My name's Dolan, and there were ten of us, boy; and it was your old man who done our family a turn none of us has ever forgotten. When my dad pushed off, sudden-like, your father — he didn't know us: he just heard about it — organised a charity benefit, put on a show, him and the other circus boys, and give the kitty to the old lady. Over a hundred quid there was. You'd be only a nipper then.

'Fill it up again, and have one yourself.'

'You have one on me — to your dad. Jeez, that was some stunt of his, that jumping over two elephants.'

'Yeah. Dadda was good.'

'That was tough about your Mum and the kid. It gimme a turn in the guts to read about it; just like they was mine, I felt.'

'Yeah.'

'Oil lamp exploded, they think.'

'Something like that.'

'I remember reading where your father got an axe and tried to belt the door in, but they dragged him away with his face all singed, and his clothes smouldering. Poor bastard. Christ, I was sorry.'

'Yeah.'

He went on talking and I went on thinking what I didn't say: He struggled terribly; he was like a madman to see; and then he just fell on the ground, them holding him, and his face crumpled: and I was frightened for him, and fell down near him, crying, and he clutched my shoulder, gripped my shoulder, and there was a bruise there for a long time after.

And there in that pub bar, in the cool stillness, his words, said a long time later, came back to me: Your mother wasn't screaming with fear for herself, but with suffering for him, a mite of two, and the way he was dying: and for you, wondering what was to become of you left behind in a world that can be so hard. I know that because I knew your mother. Well, there's nothing I can do now for young Davey, but there is a lot I can do for you.

And he saw that I got plenty to eat and a place to sleep, and a good schooling, though I left at fifteen and worked with him at different jobs in the bush and the city: and I was fierce for him, as fierce as he was for me, until it came as I see it from him looking after me to me looking after him.

This Dolan the barman was still talking, and I was pleased in a way with the memories, but he hadn't seen dadda. However, he gave me the address of a mate of my father's, Sam Chapman, and said he might be able to help me.

Old Sam had seen dadda all right; had given him shelter and a few quid, and understood he had gone to Armidale. I stayed the night with Sam, and like dadda he wanted to talk about old times. He told me things about my mother and father I didn't know: like the time they went to Centennial Park for a picnic and dadda fell in the duckpond and was arrested; and the time my mother's hat blew off in Swanston Street, Melbourne, and caused a traffic jam, while my father and a policeman chased the hat, and then wrestled for it under the body of a car and crawled out with a piece each. People roared laughing and my mother blew dadda and the policeman up in front of everybody.

At Armidale it was the same story about dadda: little bloke, had the bar in stitches; he'd jumped over two elephants, he said. And struth, you could knock him over with the wind off your spit. That's what we thought. But some stranger, big lump of a man, too, called him a liar, and the little bloke — damned if he didn't stretch him flatter than yesterday's beer. That's what the publican said.

'And last I heard he was going to Guyra. Two nights ago, it was.'

I went and had a feed and reckoned I'd push on to Guyra straightaway. My money was low, and I decided to get out on the road and try to strike a lift.

The sun went with a last slow fire burning in the trees, and nothing had passed me. Ahead two men stood by the roadside, and one was tilting a bottle to his lips. I felt that same caution I had when I was a kid and crossed to the other side of the road rather than pass big boys. And I remember my father saying to me because of that: You'll never make a man; you'll go in fear of the cowards and bullies all your life. I'll show you. And he showed me, and I remember how the nervous dread left me with the first fight I had, and how it never came back after that.

As I came abreast of the two I nodded. They partly blocked my way, and the bigger one said: 'Where you making, chum?'

'Guyra.'

'What, walking?' He was looking at the bag in my hand. 'Your car break down or something?'

'No, I haven't got a car. I'm hoping to get a lift.'

'What you going to Guyra for, all dolled up, walking?' the short one said.

'I think that's my business, mate.'

They looked at each other and the short one lit a cigarette. I watched them: young men with heavy faces, wide in the chest, with the hands of farmers; dressed like bush lairs.

The short one looked straight at me: 'You a Commo?' he said.

I gave him back his stare: 'What makes you ask that?'

'You wouldn't be a Commo going to that meeting, would yer?' the big one challenged, with a calculated blaze in his eyes

'No, I wouldn't be. I don't know what you're talking about.'

'Listen, cobber,' the big one said. 'What we're gonna do at that turnout tonight is nobody's business. We're gonna give them Commo bastards stinking hell. Get it?'

'If you're not a Commo,' said the short one, 'you'll be in it with us. Won't he, Hec?'

'My oath, that's right. Listen, the boys are picking us up here, and you can ride in with us. And you can lend a hand. The more the better.'

'No, thanks, I'll walk,' I said.

I got five yards away and they came after me, and the big one with a twisted face told me what he thought I was, and the short one swung a punch. I hit him and dropped him, and backstepped and the big one missed me with the bottle. I hooked him on the temple and let him lunge in twice, and the third time I gave it to him and that was all. His mouth was bubbling blood, and there was one of his teeth embedded in my fist. The short one lay on his belly with one arm doubled under him like the dead you see in some of those war paintings. I felt sorry, and wished I hadn't had to do it, because it was nothing to beat them.

I was walking for an hour when a car came along behind me, and skidded to a halt. The doors swung out, and men came swarming, punching and kicking, and I heard one shout: Give it to the Commo mongrel; tear his guts out! And I knew no more until I saw this girl sitting there, and a policeman, and the policeman saying what a nice job they'd made of me: broken ribs, lacerated face, fractured jaw, and asking me if I knew who did it. And I said no, I didn't remember anything.

I saw this girl many times before I was even interested in taking much notice of her. Every time I woke up she seemed to be sitting there, smiling. Then one day she came in when I was sitting up, and I watched her coming right through the ward to my bedside. She was slim, neat, in a green Donegal suit and a yellow blouse tied in a drooping bow at the neck.

'Well, hello!' she said brightly. 'Looks like the patient's coming good again at last. I knew he would.'

She had greyish-green eyes, slightly tilted, full of fun, and a little pointed chin.

'Now you'll be able to read all those magazines I've been bringing. And there's some more. And eat all those oranges. Here's some more of those, too.'

Her nose crinkled when she laughed. She pulled the yellow beret off her head and ruffled her silky brown hair with her fingers.

'You're very kind to me,' I said.

'Nonsense!'

'But you are. Why should you do this for me?'

'Why shouldn't I? You're my stray, aren't you?'

'Stray?'

'Well I was the one that found you,' she said. 'Out there on the road — just like a stray. And I put you in the car and brought you here. Impounded you, so to speak! Like me to peel you an orange?'

'No, thanks. But I'm thirteen stone. You didn't drag me into a car yourself.'

'Well, no; Dad helped. Sure you won't have an orange?'

'Okay, then.'

'You were a very sick boy. Gee, I thought you were going to die at first. Then I got the tip-off and I knew you wouldn't.'

'Tip-off? What do you mean?'

'A very special saint I've got that knows all the answers. What's your name?'

'Jim'll do.'

'Okay, Jim'll do. Mine's Aloe. We'll swap the surnames when you come out to the farm.'

'Farm? But I'm not going . . .'

'You don't think I'm going to let you convalesce here, do you? Not on your life. I'm going to see that you get really well again.'

When she was gone, and I was alone in that place of sickness it was as if a light had blinked out. I wanted to be out of there, strong in the clean air, vital as the green things growing: not sweating in the darkness thinking of him, my father, gulping the mucous that trickled back into my throat with fears for him: I wanted to be out of it, but I was a prisoner in that bed as if they had shackled me with chains.

It was good to get away to the farm, and good to feel myself getting well there. I was glad to work, for I needed the money.

The mother and father were fine people, and Aloe was perfect
— capable, sensible, affectionate, homely, and cheery as the
rise of the sun. We went to pictures and dances and had
suppers in town, and she was happy. She was like a child,
getting a great pleasure out of small joys.

She's the one to make a life with, I thought, but what can I
give her? There can be no life for me, only with my father. And
how can I take this girl into that life, asking her to share it with
a drunkard?

I told her I was leaving and she couldn't speak for a minute.
Then she said she'd drive me into the station. All too calmly
she said it. On the way she asked me suddenly: 'What's
troubling you, Jim? What's on your mind all the time?'

'Nothing.'

'You can tell me.'

'No, it wouldn't do any good.'

'Darling, I wish you would. I'd like to help. Whatever it is
I'm sure we could work it out together some way.'

I felt an impulse to tell her, but I didn't. She stopped the car
at the station, and I grabbed her in my arms. The way she
kissed me I never wanted to let her go.

'You'll come back, won't you?'

'No, Aloe. It's got to finish here.'

'I've got a hunch it won't'

'Another tip-off?'

'Uh-huh.'

'Some saint, that bloke.'

She laughed: 'And if you don't, I'm going after you, so there.
And I mean it. You're not going to get away from me — ever.'

She wouldn't come on to the platform. She drove away. I
could have smashed every silly face in that carriage. I was
upset about everything. I kept seeing her kitten face; and I
could remember my mother saying goodbye to my father at
the station when he had to go away, and I had an idea how he
must have felt; and she must have felt something like Aloe.

I wondered about that gang of anti-communist demonstrators who beat me up, and I thought how easy for the innocent to be hurt by the stupidity of hatred. I was too young for the war, but I saw men marching away. I heard the count of the dead, the wounded, the widows and orphans. I saw men marching back, and I heard the big mouths prating: Let us not forget our glorious dead; while they forgot their glorious living. I read of agony and sorrow: families torn up like bits of paper and lost forever to one another.

It could be like this with you, I thought. Maybe it could be that your father was one of them, and you looking for him, even now, here, in this country.

But no — there's no looking over barbed wire for him, not here; no kicking of the heaps of human bones and wondering if his are there; no peering into the chambers where the living were herded to die, or sighting for him among the walking dead, meeting and passing him, not knowing him the way he is. Thinking of it like that I felt the gorge come up in me and my mind striking out like a bird flown into a house and blundering for the light, to escape; praying: Christ, come to earth, walk the cities of this world, and the towns; preach from the halls and the hillsides, and help us; for the love of God, give us love and understanding.

I was shaking and nearly crying. A man gets worked up, and I was worked up then.

I found no sign of dadda in the Northern River towns, but I heard about him in the canefield country, and I followed every lead, but he was always gone when I got there. And the clues to his identity were always the same: A little man with mighty shoulders: a short joker who says he jumped over two elephants.

It's a strange thing, indeed, I thought, to be following a man as if he were a fugitive and you a detective; it's a queer thing the restlessness on him that makes him keep wandering, retracing the pattern of his movements of yesterday: dawdling the main streets of a dozen towns, finding a memory in the swing of a light, the lettering of a sign, the arrangement of the sky about a building: noons and midnights and dawns marking a time and place for him.

At Mungindi I saw the spot where the big top had been, and my mind went back in a flash: How clean those elephants, scrubbed with long-handled brushes, their yellow toenails filed like horn, their foreheads painted with red and white triangles: standing now girth to girth. The warbs running in and bolting down the springboards, one on each side of the animals: the ringmaster posing dramatically and spacing his syllables; the clamour of the kettledrums.

And dadda appearing — in dove-grey tights with a scarlet cummerbund, the muscles gliding on his shoulders and arms: gauging his distance: the gallop of the drums: running, running, bouncing on the first plank, not a foot from the ground, shooting into the air in three somersaults over the elephants' backs, landing on the opposite plank, bouncing twice, and then returning in three back somersaults to lob triumphant on the first shaking board. Over in a minute, but a sensation, and the roaring going on for minutes after he left the ring.

It was a feat that acrobats might laugh at now; maybe it's tame to them with the dangerous stunts they've perfected, but it was a great thing when dadda did it. It was original and brilliant. And somehow the massiveness of those elephants made him look even shorter than he was, so that the magnitude of his jump was intensified, and that put the crowd on his side.

I went on in the same way, but working here and there, and I was hearing about dadda in the same way. And then with changes. I was hearing about him like this: Shabby sorta coot; looked like he never had a wash for a week: He was here, the boots off his feet; I give him a pair and a feed and a few bob: He slept all night out in the open; poked in here with frost on his clothes. And I knew I'd find him soon after that.

It was in Tamworth. A publican said he'd seen him going along the road out of town, pretty full. I took the road, watching, listening in the gathering dusk. He was sitting drawn up against a stump near a clearing. He looked little and old, sick and dishevelled. But he still had the shoulders.

'What's the matter?' I greeted him. 'Look as if you lost a quid and found sixpence.'

He lifted his head, peering, and let it loll again: 'Go ter hell. I dunno you.'

I stood above him, looking down, and thinking: Your father, fifty-odd years of time on him, and a little while ago he was like you. Cherish him, not because blood is thicker than water, but because he was a good man that believed in good men. Look with his eyes at the deserted years to be, and the full years behind, gone, and nothing to do but live in a cave of the spirit with them, and fetch them out and look at them like treasured things from an old trunk nobody else gives a damn about and never looks into.

'You know me all right, dadda. Jim.'

'No, you're not Jim,' he said hoarsely.

I grabbed him under the armpits, but he shook himself free, and he cried fiercely: 'To hell with you! Get away if you're Jim, you mug. I'm no good to you. For Christ's holy sake, will you get away!'

I tried again to lift him, but he was raging, and it enraged me to see him: Never mind that you're no good for me, I thought. My mother loved you, but she wouldn't know you now. I'm not seeing you rot. She wouldn't, and I'm not. You've got to be good — for you. You're going to pull out of this, and get on your feet, and be the man you really are inside you.

'Get on your feet, dadda — and no capers now.'

He was like a sack to pick up, but I got an arm around him and walked him slowly away from there; and he said nothing, only kept snivelling softly. There was a great savagery of grief on me at his dereliction. I felt suddenly alone, and in need of someone to turn to, but there was no hope. Only Aloe. And I kept thinking of her. For strength I kept thinking of Aloe.

She seemed to be about me in the stillness and starlight, her warmth and her words; and I wanted her to be. I wanted to hold her in my mind.

What can I do? Look, is it right?

This man with me is broken, and where am I taking him? He is my father that I searched for, and suffered for, and found. But where are we going: To a train, a city, a shabby room in a slum. Back to the beginning; into the rut. And him with even less of his manhood left, more helpless than ever before. There is no solution there; there is nothing, only decay, and the perpetuation of decay. All that I've gone through — what will it avail me, what will it avail him, if we return?

No, I will go back to Aloe, and maybe, she will have the answer. Maybe we can indeed work out something together, a new way of life that will make the last of your days, dadda, as good as the first. But she will see you the way you are, in every stark detail the way you are. Nothing will be concealed to bias her decision. I will tell her the story, my part of it — but you, with your jumping over two elephants and all that that signifies: you will tell her that, and she will judge you by it. And if the judgement's good maybe you'll go on to tell it even to my sons.

INTO THE SILENCE

*T*he noise became a big wheel spinning, pounding, humming. There was the fright of crashing mountains in it and the pace of comets. There was an agony of terror. And then it seemed the house flew apart like flowers in a high wind, and the noise was gone. And when he saw it was gone, he went over and sat on the bed and simpered. He folded his arms, the hands crushed under the armpits and rocked back and forth, moaning a little. He sat there for a long time.

When he got up he stood for a moment, and walked to the door leading out of the bedroom and suddenly on the threshold turned his face in fear. But there was no need. He made a little cautious noise in his throat, and backed away down the hall. He went into the kitchen, and took food from the cupboard, a muttonbone, and started to wrest the meat off it. He was tearing off the heel of a loaf when he stopped, listening, with the bread still in his mouth and a sweat of alarm on his forehead.

He crept back along the hall towards the bedroom, and standing pressed against the wall held the bread in his outstretched hand in the doorway. His mouth was open, waiting. But there was no sound. He stood square in the

177

doorway and ate the bread, and there was no sound, and he stared in wonderment and perplexity.

Then he made sure. He cried out: 'I will take the food and eat the food, and I will keep away from no one! I will not stay in this house, and I will eat all the food that I can put in my belly!'

And when he said these words he waited in dread. But nothing happened. He made doubly sure. He went to the forbidden drawer and pulled out of it the guarded treasures — the trinkets and the photographs and the doyleys and flung them scattered on the floor. His heart was like a great bird in the cage of his chest as he watched and waited, but nothing happened.

Slowly the little sounds came out of his throat and the light broke across his understanding, gradually melting the last lingering shadows of his incredulity.

The noise was gone.

Sitting there, thinking, his hands came into focus, and he lifted them up and turned them this way and that: but he didn't see the thick wrists, the padded palms, the hair-bronzed joints, the burred knuckles. He saw them as hollow gloves; the noise had gone into them. He slapped them upturned and downturned on the bed, and struck them against the wall, skinning them, but no noise came and he knew the noise wasn't in them.

He was full of joy. He went back into the kitchen and ate bread and butter and drank milk. He saw the packet of cigarettes on the shelf and he took one for the first time in his life and struck a match to light it. He puffed at the cigarette, but held it away and scrutinised it with a look of distaste. Then he thought there was pleasure in crushing it out. He held the lighted end in the saucer and pressed down, and the cigarette bent and crumpled with a twist. He liked that. He lit all the cigarettes and put them out that way.

He went into his little room and fell asleep on the stretcher. He came out of sleep in the darkness, and jumped up and ran to the door listening for footfalls; and pelting back and turning on the kitchen light, and standing aghast at the dirt and neglect, he swiftly cleared the table, shoving the dishes in the sink, and putting on the tablecloth, and pulling potatoes out of the vegetable box and hurrying to peel them.

Then he remembered what he remembered this morning. He went on working, but he didn't hurry. There was a bright calm on his face. He ate the meal and defiantly left the dishes, and went back to bed. He lay awake in the darkness, and the creak of the house was strange in the darkness as the darkness was strange in the creak of the house. He knew the sound of the iron roof shrinking, the weatherboards stretching, the floor boards talking like mice among themselves. The tap dripped like a little mallet on glass and the window across from him shrugged loosely in its frame. He knew all these things that had been with him a thousand nights, but tonight they were strange.

He went to sleep when sleep took him like a drug. But he woke in darkness, and sat bolt upright in terror. He jumped out of bed and ran through the house putting on the lights. He was stark naked, the way he always slept, the way he always had to sleep, and the hair glinted redly on his chest and belly and was a tumbled shaggy flare on his head. His thick shoulders hunched as he stood there, with his long shadow up the hall like a wet stain on the faded carpet. The slight currents of air touched and turned chill the sweat on his body, raising a rough Braille on his flesh.

At five o'clock in the evening he heard footsteps crunching on the gravel walk, and wild-eyed, shaggy-headed, he ran down the hall and pulled the key out of the door. A woman was framed in the keyhole, walking up to the keyhole, then a check wall against the keyhole.

She knocked. He didn't move his head. His lip curled slightly. She knocked again, and then again: 'Yoo-hoo. Anyone home?'

'Go away,' he said, frightened by the voice.

'That you, Toby?' the woman said, with a note of greeting in her voice. 'Where's your mother?'

'Go away.'

'She's not sick, or something, is she?'

He didn't answer, and she said sharply, with anger: 'The boss wants to know why she wasn't at work yesty, or today. Tell her I want to see her at once.'

Still he didn't answer, and he heard her angry voice as if she were pressing her mouth to the wood: 'If you don't speak to me and do as I say I'll tell her when I see her, and you know what that'll mean for you. Are you going to tell me?'

She waited, and he waited, and she said: 'All right, my lad.'

He watched her shrink in the keyhole again. Halfway down the path she turned her white, wrinkled face and looked back. He saw her thin mouth and squinted eyes. He watched her go through the gate and past the keyhole.

And suddenly he felt the exhaustion of the day's search and the day's vigilance. He felt the weakness in his bowels, a sick emptiness, and he cringed away from the conqueror: the noiseless noise sheltering in the stillness, hiding in the silence; and he was crying his submissiveness, cowering, and mouthing his obedience, saying: 'I will be good, I will be good. I won't steal no more food when you're away. I won't answer no doors. I will keep inside.'

He started sobbing in a terrible contrition, slobbering in his hands and rocking his head wildly. Slowly he stopped. He kept very quiet. He sat very still.

As if a light had poured into his brain, he knew where the noise was. He knew where it was, and he knew why it wouldn't start, because the words had to start it. The words had to start it, and the words had to leave off being words and become only sound, and the sound build fast and heavy and become the big wheel spinning, roaring like the whirl of atoms and terrible in its velocity.

The noise was not gone out of that house. It was still in that house, hidden away somewhere in the silence. It was around.

It waited unheard and watched unseen. It was with him. Like a man who walks in fear of coming upon an armed quarry, he crept through the house, listening, listening with a strained alertness for its whereabouts.

It was laired in that silence, and he sought clues from the silence. He looked up in the darkish corners of the roof among the wisps of cobweb bearded with dust as if he might see it there. He scouted under the bed and behind the plain cheap wardrobe, looking and listening; he went into the other bedroom, and stood stock still when he saw the whip on the floor. His teeth started to chatter with ferocity. He ran out of the room and slammed the door shut. He was shivering.

Then the silence was all around him as around a statue; he heard the wash of it in his ears. He went into the kitchen and stared all around, knowing it was looking at him and knowing that he might surprise it grimacing from behind the tins on the top of the dresser, leering from under the table, sitting with cunning secrecy, like a sniper, on the broken light shade above his head. But he saw and heard nothing. Rage came snarling out of his horror. He wanted the silence to be shaped, shaped so he could beat it into confessing the whereabouts of the noise.

But there was no way he could handle it. Fright and horror strengthened in him.

This was not like yesterday, when the chains were broken, the house no longer a barricade and he could dwell on the pleasant instincts of freedom. He hadn't vanquished the noise; he'd only hidden it and now he couldn't find it. He feared its power more than ever because it was unseen and unexpectant.

He fled into his room and shut the door and fell on the bed.

In a little while he heard another noise, and he listened to it — the light slap of running feet, the clink of bottles on the verandah, the feet again, and silence. He put out the light and looked through the window. A misty man was running along the street in the dawn.

He went and opened the front door, put his hand around and

181

picked up the milk. He drank one bottle of it in a frightened way, as though trying to lure the sound out of its silence. He went back to his bedroom, and lay there, tortured, and started moaning.

He ran into the bedroom and fell down where the noise was cooped: where he thought it was cooped, and where he had to prove it was cooped; so that by proving it to be there he would prove it to be nowhere else.

He punched and tugged, and pulled and slapped, and shouted: 'Idiot, ape and beast. Say the words, say the words, say them, say them, say them!'

But the silence was only the more clam-lipped and deeper for the sound from himself: his screeching voice, his harsh panting, the fleshy cuffings of his hands, the bumping of the head on the floor.

Say them, say the words. You did this and I told you not to. You didn't do this and I told you to do it. You lying thief. Mongrel. To think that you should ever come from me. Say them! You bastard, you'll pay for it; I'll make you pay for it. Say the words, say them, say them. I don't care if you say them, but say them!

He was weeping, shrieking, but the deaf don't hear and the dumb don't speak and the dead are deaf and dumb. He saw a black, shiny boot, and blue serge, and he shot his head up wildly, and the policeman was staring down at him, at his crumpled face, the grey hair in his clutching hands, and the heavy, masculine woman with the frozen snarl whose body he sat astride.

THE GINGER GIANT

*T*his Cody Codrington, that was called The Ginger
Giant, had a grandmother that would put her fists up to a man
when she felt like it. And give him something to go on with,
too. She was a Tipperary woman. You will remember her when
I say the name: Katie Brigid McGarrigle. You remember how
they used to talk about her — those boxers, wrestlers, and
sports writers — in the saloon bar of the Cock and Bull or The
Bent Elbow, and say what a grand old tiger she was, and didn't
she knock Jack Dunleavy down in a spar one time, though
some will argue that Dunleavy wasn't really trying, and had a
big wink in his eye when he fell.

And you know how I told you that in the Harp of Erin,
around where she lived, Dermott McDowell, the publican
who did time for refusing to stand up for the king at the
pictures, had a photo of her on the wall near Carbine, and a
poor sod came in there one day and said a word against her and
they carried him out. It was like calling Les Darcy, God rest his
young soul, a muddleheaded boy in a Maitland pub, and you
know where calling Les Darcy a muddleheaded boy in a
Maitland pub can get you, don't you? That's right.

Well, when they came down from the bush to live in the city, this fighting grandmother of Cody Codrington's was near sixty, with a face crinkled like a spinach leaf, and just enough teeth to hold a little clay pipe. There must have been a time when Cody had a mother and father, but he couldn't remember them. All he could remember was his gran telling him stories, feeding him porridge, spuds, and extract of beef; sitting up all night with him and his fever in lamplight; flaying him with soap and water behind his ears; taking him to school on his first day — and teaching him to fight: all because he came home crying one day and saying a big boy who looked like James J. Jeffries had given him a shock, a shiner, and a busted lip.

'And you turned tail and run, did you?' she said.

'I did not; I tried to fight him,' said Cody.

'Come in here.'

She took the six-year-old boy into the spare room, and shaped up; she asked him to show her how he had tackled the boy like James J. Jeffries. He came in tapping at first because he was bewildered and afraid of hurting her; but she jeered at him for his baby blows, and banged him on the nose, and jibed: Gah, you couldn't beat pussy.

Cody snarled, and flurried in hammering, and jerking out: I'll show you if I can't beat pussy. She dodged and weaved and backstepped and blocked, and hit him, and the harder she hit him the more savagely he bored in, until he was crying with rage, loud and fierce, and punching wildly; all the time her eyes were gleaming with pride and excitement. There was a smile curled like the flourish of a pen on her lips.

When he was nearly out on his feet with exhaustion, scarlet-eared and bloody-nosed, she said, panting: That's a good boy, no more. You've the mettle all right, and you'll beat anything.

She taught him, not out of books, because she said she knew more than ever came out of books.

There were six boys and a girl in our family, she said, and I was the girl. You don't live with six teasing, pranking larrikins without learning how to take care of yourself. And my dadda, he was the one with the fists, and could have been a great champion in the ring only for getting an eye poked out in a brawl over the Government: and that told to him by no less a person than Mike McTigue himself. I sparred with him, and with my six brothers, who were fighting men; I sparred with Terry McGovern, too, believe it if you like. I saw them doing their training, the silk of them, and all their fights, and there's not much I don't know about the game, she said.

She told Cody great tales of great men of the ring, and there wasn't a fight she didn't take him to see. They had permanent seats at the Stadium. She would make Cody study the styles of the fighters, and then at home analyse them for him and show where in her estimation they had fallen short. With Cody the fight game became an obsession. He had it for breakfast, dinner, and tea, and he went to bed with it. He sailed home in school tournaments, and when he left school he beat everything in the amateurs, and nothing stood up to him for more than a few rounds in the preliminaries.

Will Lawless, you know, that wrote for *The Referee* saw him and wrote up his prospects, saying he looked like a coming champion. And remember that great little pug, Billy Fidler? He saw Cody when he was in this country, and he said he was the goods, and he called him The Ginger Giant, and the name stuck, for that's what Cody was: powerfully built and tall with it, and with a great shaggy shock of auburn hair that seemed to reflect in his pale pink face and body.

Billy the Fidler, as the Aussies tagged him, said more than that. He said of Katie McGarrigle that she was the best coach and trainer in Australia. She had the instinctive wisdom for spotting the good in a boy and developing it. The papers printed that, and there was a great fuss one way and another: letters to the editors from other trainers, and members of parliament and clergymen saying a woman's place was in the home and not in the prize ring, and feminist societies choking over their tea and biscuits, so fast did their tongues mag with pride in their sex.

When Cody went in among the challengers Katie really gave the tongues something to talk about. She believed in solid roadwork, and she got an old bike and pedalled after the jogging Cody every morning. She got him on to the hard yakka that the pugs of the old school, like Cribb and Gully, and Sayers, took in their stride. So it was that Cody Codrington had more stamina than the Melbourne express, and could run up a hill full pelt and stand at the top asking for more. His brine-soaked hands were like rocks, and he was so tough he could squeeze a goat to death.

She put on the gloves with him at home, in a backyard ring, under a marquee; and did the hiring of sparring partners. She had to turn the crowds away. At the Stadium she was his chief second, advising him and shouting ballyhooly at the delighted crowd, who taunted her with such remarks as: Tell him to use the underarm one, Mum. And: Hey, Granny, lend him your hatpin.

But that was only at the beginning. As the elimination contests were run off and the challengers went down, one after another, the fight public developed a respect and a great liking for Katie McGarrigle, and anyone that threw a jeer often found himself belted by half the bleachers. She became a well-known figure everywhere, and was loved and admired as the mascot of a great and beloved sport of this country.

Cartoonists showed Katie with a pipe in her mouth, her grey hair in a bun and her diminutive frame enveloped in black bloomers boxing with the towering Cody. The sports writers told of Cody's green trunks and the holy medals sewn in the waistline; when they walked down the street, or to their duty of a Sunday, the red-haired giant with the swinging stride and the door-width shoulders, and the little peewit of a woman in black, there were nods and smiles and good-days all the way.

When Cody Codrington won the championship that night to an ocean of sound Katie McGarrigle jumped into the ring and hugged him, and the cameras flashed, and four burly heavies carried them both to Cody's dressing room with the crowd cheering to lift the roof. Back at the house there was a grand party, a parlor full, with the grappler known as Neck-Buster Kelly making the piano bend in the middle, and the voices bawling out the old Irish songs to make your chest rise like dough under your chin and sting your eyes with pride and joy: and Punchy O'Reilly running in to say there was a streetful of people and telling them to stop and listen; and they did, and the choir of voices was carrying on the song out in the street.

Next day telegrams poured in; one was from the Governor-General himself, and another from Nat Fleisher in America. An old man came with a gold medal, and on this medal was engraved: For Clancy Tobin, a good man, the best with his fists on the Ballarat Diggings. And the old man said that was his dad; he was killed in the ructions at Eureka. He wanted Cody to have the medal that was the greatest treasure he had. Cody beat the next two challengers for his title in a few rounds. There was nothing could stop him, it seemed; he'd be champ of the world yet.

But Katie McGarrigle was a little worried. He was young, and adulation could lead him into temptation. There were women like peacocks who could put a spell on a man with a look of the eye, and they were no good. There were leeches and spongers and party-throwers and grog-bibbers and the types that wanted to get close to him and go along with him under his umbrella of greatness, the crusaders of high living and quick dying. That, thought Katie, was the worst that could happen to Cody.

She was wrong.

Cody kept his head, and it was home by the fire and early to bed with him, but what happened to Cody was this: He went up to the Blue Mountains for a weekend and came home talking about a girl that he'd met there. Katie McGarrigle looked at his smiling face and glossy eyes, and then up at the photo of John L. on the wall, and thought: You big blockhead, I told you to look after him. But she went on smoking her cutty, with narrowed eyes.

'We came home together,' Cody said. 'In the train. She speaks beautiful, and knows a lot about many things. She works at the University.'

Katie looked suspicious. Had this one been feeding her boy a fancy line?

'She knew you, did she?'

'No, she didn't,' Cody said. 'And I didn't tell her. She's an Oriental scholar, I think she called it. She says Ireland is older than China.'

'Big and fat or thin and old?'

Cody Codrington laughed at the glint in his grandmother's eyes: 'She's twenty,' he said. 'With little bones and hair as black as your umbrella, only bright, like treacle, and so small she only comes up to here on me.' He tapped his chest. 'She was saying about Edmund Burke, you know the great magsman you've told me about, that he had a dead ringer in a great Chinese orator called Shun Tang who lived away back in some dynasty or another. She did say, but I don't remember.'

'She's keen on finding the relationship between pigtails and shillelaghs, I must say,' muttered Katie, an uneasy feeling working up in her. 'Will you be seeing her again?'

'Tomorrow, I told her.'

'Fetch her home for a bite, if you like,' Katie said, wanting to see this siren who'd turned the head of Cody Codrington — her baby, boy and man these last twenty years.

So it came about, and Katie McGarrigle got the shock of her life, as who doesn't when the completely unexpected turns up?

Cody came down the hall hallooing, and Katie hurried in from the kitchen, hawk-eyed, peering past him. Cody turned, smiling, and said: Gran, this is Judy. And, Judy, this is my grandmother, the best in the world.

Katie McGarrigle's mouth fell open with surprise; she looked from one to the other as though Cody were having her on. Suddenly she was aware that the girl had spoken in a voice like windbells, saying how pleased she was to meet her. Katie thought she had better say something, and she said: Come in and make yourself at home.

She took the girl's hat and coat, and saw the girl had a figure like a vase, smooth and shapely. She didn't like this a bit. She couldn't think of what to say. It was as if the words had been chased out of her with the astonishment.

The girl sat down, neat as sixpence, and Cody roared up the stairs to have a wash, and came down singing and so full of joy that he didn't see the look on Katie's face. She excused herself and went out to the kitchen to get on with the tea. When Cody bowled out a few minutes afterwards, asking if she wanted a good man for the carving of the chook, she took his ear and pulled his head down to her and hissed: 'You didn't tell me she was a Chinese.'

'Only a half-caste she is,' Cody said, grinning.

'And what's the other half of her?' snapped Katie. 'You must be out of your head.'

'But why?' His blue eyes rounded innocently.

'If you want a girl keep to your own, why don't you?' flashed Katie McGarrigle.

'Ah, come on, Gran, don't be tough now. Just think, maybe she's got contacts, and she'll be able to get you some opium to smoke in that little pipe of yours.' He laughed rumbustiously.

Katie's face kept its gravity: 'It's not funny a bit,' she snapped. But he went on tickling her ribs, until she gave him a belt over the ear that sent him laughing away.

But Katie wasn't joking and she made it clearer that she opposed Cody's going steady with a Chinese girl — for all her beauty, the red lips like cut strawberries, and the olive skin, and the tilted brown eyes, and the mind that could make dummies of professors. She had nothing personal against the girl, she would point out, but lemons and apples don't mix, do they? Surely, God knows, there were plenty of his race to pick from; you'd never go short there. A good Australian girl, with the temperament to match, and the ways of ordinary people — that was what he ought to be after.

'But I've not seen any to me fancy,' Cody explained, worried and disappointed that his grandmother didn't approve of the girl. 'Where are they? Do they grow on bushes, and you just pluck them and say: Right, we're a pair of turtle doves, let's coo. I like this girl, and it's great fun to be with her, and I don't see what her being Chinese has got to do with it.'

But Katie wouldn't relent, presenting an ever-harder surface of implacable disapproval. Underneath, though, it seemed to her that if Cody was happy that was all that mattered. She knew as well as anybody else that he could have picked up with the whitest-skinned girl in the country and have a dog's life with her. But she never gave ground to him. She told him there was always the chance of his getting a suitable girl who was right in every way, and in the long run he'd be happier with her because he was on his own territory and not setting foot on foreign soil where everything was different, from the food you ate to the prayers you said. She never let up on him. She taunted and teased him about Judy, and when he wanted to speak of her she pretended not to be interested.

When he came home that night in August she was sitting with her feet to the fire, knitting. He sat down on the stool nearby, and she said: 'Well, has she got you believing Saint Patrick was a Chinaman yet?'

'Gran,' said Cody Codrington. 'Judy and me are going to get married.'

The knitting dropped in her lap.

'In a month,' said Cody. 'I'm going to fix it all up tomorrow. In Saint Mary's, it'll be. Performed by Archbishop Kelly himself.'

'Cody,' she said. 'You're going to tell me in a minute I'm as mad as a meataxe for believing you.'

'But it's true, Gran. I mean it.'

She stood up, white-faced and walked around the table, and turned to see him smiling at her: 'Oh, you fool of a feller,' she said. Then she shot at him: 'I won't give me consent.'

'I'm over 21,' grinned Cody.

'I'll tell Hughie Kelly himself to stop it or he's no friend of mine.'

Cody sprang up and walked over and hugged her, saying: 'It'll be a grand affair, Mrs. McGarrigle, and you'll be the most beautiful grandma there. Will you help me with the arranging, with the breakfast that I'd like to put on at Gregorys', or maybe Sheedys', or one of the other big places, but which I'd like better to put on here in this house, homely and all as it is. Will you, Gran?'

'Seeing you've made up your mind,' Katie said, matter-of-factly, 'I wish you well, but I'll not be at your wedding, Cody. I'll help, yes, and I will be hostess here, but I'll not be at your wedding.'

Cody couldn't understand her logic, but it seemed right to her. She couldn't appear at a marriage she opposed. That was hypocritical. But helping with the breakfast and looking after the guests — that was only like being a servant.

And so Judy Loy and Cody Codrington were married. The Cathedral was crowded, and the confetti from the crowd outside was like a snowstorm. A thunder of cheering went up right back into Hyde Park. Press photographers and newsreel cameramen mixed with coppers and boxers with battered ears, and aldermen, and insurance agents, and — well, I don't know who wasn't there. You couldn't see the cars for flowers; they looked like floats. And there were times when Cody was near to crying like a great big pup.

At home Katie McGarrigle raged around, telling John L. Sullivan, Ike O'Neil Weir, James J. Corbett and the rest of them on the dining room wall what a shameful old crow she was, and then wailing to them that she couldn't help feeling the way she did.

The telephone kept ringing with congratulations, and the telegram boy, it seemed, was no sooner away than he was back again. And then the great wrestler, Kosciusko Cox, that was so big you'd rather jump over than walk around him, appeared behind an enormous horseshoe bouquet of flowers; when Katie answered the door his bristly head shot through his horseshoe, and he said coyly and shyly blushing: 'For the bride and groom from the boys. I beat up three dozen ginks gettin' 'em here, Katie, and yer can tell Cody that, and he'll know what we think of him.'

It was a great do they had, singing and music and funny stories, so clean soap wasn't in it: the place stuffed with people, and everybody helping himself, eating on the wing, nursing his drink and in no time making the great table look like grasshopper time outback. Judy's parents put in an appearance, more as a formality for they left early, although that could have been because they felt uncomfortable and didn't fit in too well with the company. Katie, in the hustle and bustle, saw so little of them it seemed like a peepshow, and then when she was all set for a good garp they had gone.

At two in the morning it wound up, and Cody and his bride went off to the honeymoon hotel, where they would leave from next day for Brisbane and the Barrier Reef. After they'd gone Katie and Charlie the Feather, Paddington Smith and McDowell from The Harp and a few others got good and drunk: and McDowell sang The Emigrant's Song, and Katie McGarrigle was glad because she could cry, and put everything into the cry, and lie that she could never hear that song without going to pieces.

After that she was never quite the same with Cody. She might have been; she might have let the chip fall off her shoulder, might have cast out the rock of stubbornness in her heart — the stubborness that stands like a castle in the Irish and is both a vice and a virtue of the race — had she not gone that afternoon to Cody's new place.

It was just after he came back from his honeymoon. He called for her in a taxi, and he talked to her all the way, telling of the time he'd had: of the wonders of the Reef, and how there is an animal there that has the patience of Job and lives for nothing else but to build a coral underworld: and starting some parts of it when the fellers with iron knuckle-dusters were doing their stuff in front of Nero and putting the finishing touches to those parts just now.

'They've the art of sticking together no matter who's running the world up above at the time,' he said. 'And they don't chop and change their natures with the ages; nor their customs, nor their fashions.

Judy had been prating to him, Katie knew, and that was his manner of recapitulation.

Cody told Katie of the reception he got from Brisbane north when people knew who he was; and did she see the papers? And how he ran across Patsy Pearce, the Pride of Carpentaria, the man who floored Flash Jack Johnson in a backyard spar at the Sir Joseph Banks; living in a dosshouse now, sick more often than not, but still selling the tale for a crust and a drink.

'He wished with all the warmth in him to be remembered to you.'

Cody gabbled on, but Katie didn't seem to be interested. She nodded, smiled vaguely. She did not ask him questions, though he wanted that. He wanted her to share in his knowledge and in his enjoyment. Her lack of interest dampened his spirit, and he fell silent.

But she had seen the papers all right. She had grabbed at every bit of news about him and his trip, though appearing to be indifferent. There were a few on the inside, close to her, ones like McDowell and Paddington Smith, who knew the truth: how she was anxious that everything go along happily with nobody poking borak at Cody's choice in wives, shooting jibes and veiled insults. And they knew that every time she looked at the news pictures of him among the crowds at railway stations, hotels, or in public halls, she studied the printed faces, looking for signs of contempt and derision, and wondering what those people were really feeling and thinking and saying; for people talk, she'd say, and people must have talked about Cody and his Chinese bride. And the shame of it all burned her again with its anguish.

Then they were at Cody's place, and straightaway, from the outside Katie McGarrigle appraised it as much too grand a place for the simple boy she had reared; and when she stepped inside she was even more convinced, and moreover she knew she had made a mistake in coming.

For the place was full of Chinese, of all shapes and sizes and ages: the smaller and the younger turning out to be Judy's three brothers and sister, all scrubbed clean and smiling; and the elder Judy's mother and father, her uncle, aunt, and grandmother, who couldn't speak English, only shake her head vigorously and chirp like a bird. In fact, the piping and shrilling of the whole company sounded to Katie McGarrigle like an aviary; and at no other time in her life was she more surrounded by so many sparkling eyes and so many sets of teeth flashing in her direction.

Cody's wife sought to take her hat, but Katie said it was doing no harm where it was, and full of a shocked and bewildered uneasiness she sat down as gingerly as if the chair was garnished with prickly pear.

In a minute the hospitality was laid on. There was wine, water and lemonade. There was cake and fruit. There was a Persian cat getting around like the Queen of Sheba, using the McGarrigle hosiery to give itself a currycomb and now and then bending a snob's eye on the glass tank alive with coloured fishes. There was a warmth of luxury, and the talk was a skirl and a bumble like a pub when the mob's there. To Katie it seemed that all China had cut loose with the gift of speech.

As she looked and listened the gall spilled into her mind; with distress and horror she wondered how it was that she was here amid all this foreignness; at the same time answering herself that it was all supposed to be part and parcel of her life now — a linkage of strangers, a brand new heap of relatives that had no more place in her life than a banana on the Apple and Pear Board.

The gorge that rose in her was no better for the conviction

that Cody had brought her here with the shrewd idea of giving her a knockdown to the folks he'd come by free and for nothing and so getting off to a good start in the first leg of the happy family circle.

Well, poor Cody had another think coming.

Katie McGarrigle stood up so suddenly that the cake plate fell off her lap.

'If you'll excuse me,' said Katie, 'I'll be taking me leave now.'

There was a hush, and then the voices pealed out again: not so soon, surely; why she had only just come; you must stay a while longer, and all that.

Katie could not control the trembling of her lips, the outrage that pinched her face white and steeled her eye.

'I mean no offence,' she said. 'But I'm not one to put on a front. I'll say what's in me, and it's this. I know me place, and it's not here. Me mother was Irish, me father was Irish, and I am Irish, too. I've nothing against you people; you're as good as the next. But each to his own, I say, and I'll stick to mine. Thanks to you for the tea and the cake. Good afternoon.'

And with that, her gaze brittle and her lips firm, she swept to the door. Cody stood there, his face a blank with unresolved thoughts.

'Gran . . .' he started.

She glared at him as she passed.

'How could you?' she said. 'How could you do this to us?' Then she was gone.

Well, as I said, she was never quite the same with Cody again after that. She still managed him and seconded his fights, but she was never keen to hear of his home-life with his wife. It stuck in his gizzard, too. In that way they grew apart, though Cody came to see her now and again. She never visited him.

He was at the peak of his fighting form, and belted two importations from America and one from the Philippines. Some were egging him to go overseas and have a crack at the world title, but he was happy where he was for a while. Then a son was born to him, a black-haired nipper, with Cody's big bones and just an echo of his mother's tilted eyes.

Katie didn't see the child until he was a year old, when Cody brought him to the house. And she didn't say much, though secretly she was proud. Judy, Cody's wife, didn't come. She never did. She knew when she wasn't welcome, though she harboured no grudge. They called the boy Barney, and when Barney was nearly three and his father was still holding the championship and Katie McGarrigle's shoulders had stooped a little more, Cody's wife died in childbirth, the infant with her.

Katie answered a knock on the door at three in the morning, and there was Cody, face drawn and eyes wild, with Barney wrapped and asleep in his arms. He said dully: 'Judy's dead.' And went through into the dining room, and put the boy on the couch and sat with his head on the table, saying: 'I can't believe it. I still can't believe it.' He started to cry.

Standing back, Katie swallowed, still trembling with shock, come once again to that time in her life when what is said is nothing and there is nothing to say. She put a hand on Cody's shoulder, and said: 'I am sorry.'

He muttered strangely: 'Are you?'

She noticed it: 'I am, indeed.'

It was as if he felt now the real impact of her resentment against his wife; as if his disappointment had boiled up in bitterness, and he wanted to relieve his helpless sorrow: 'Don't be giving me sympathy,' he said. 'I don't want it. She's gone and there's no bringing her back. You never liked her and you don't have to change now.'

With a wild flurry of words he told her he didn't know what he was saying, and he was sorry, and he couldn't stick to sitting around; he had to get out and walk the pain out of himself. Katie let him go out into the night, and stood there looking down at the sleeping child, helpless.

There's some can tell you better than I can how Cody went to the pack after that. He was a dead man living. You know that feller that was always shouting Passchaendale whenever he got lit up in the Cricketers' Arms, and how we saw his hair changing color till it was white in a few weeks? It was the same with Cody Codrington. That great shock of red hair of his turned grey with a pink tinge in it; like the mane of a lion it was. Talk to him for half an hour and you'd suddenly wake up that he'd said hardly a word; he hadn't even heard. He refused to fight any more. He retired and the title was left vacant.

It was no kidstakes with Cody Codrington. He was never the type to parade his emotions for the sake of self-pity and the encouragement of sympathy. What hit him hit him hard and knocked him down. And when he got up the effects of the blow were still there.

Then he went bush. He left his boy with his wife's people and put up a swag and hit the road. It didn't take much thought to know why he struck out that way. He wanted to get away from people that knew him, from the old environment with all its torments and into one entirely different yet one that he had known for a time as a boy. More than anything he wanted to get away from himself.

Nobody could say Katie McGarrigle didn't fret, though Katie didn't let on what she felt. Where he was, what he was doing, how he was getting on — that's what worried her. The silence of his absence tortured her with anxiety. She used to watch for the postman, Clever Riley, every day, with the blind drawn back to sight his approach and falling into place when he passed. She asked McDowell and Paddington Smith and everyone else if they'd heard anything: not in a straight way, but in a casual gossipy style as if Cody was just down the street and it was getting late and it's a wonder what's keeping him all this time.

But the months went by and there was no word of Cody. Everyone was losing patience with him on account of Katie, the way he was hurting her and how it was a shame to see it. At The Harp one day McDowell said: 'A man ought to put the police on to him. There's no knowing whether he's dead or alive. A little bit of a scrawl to tell us he's all right, that's all we want.'

He told Katie, but she said to him if he brought the police in she'd never speak to him again. McDowell was one man who cared about that, who would never get over the cut of not having Katie McGarrigle talk to him for the rest of his life.

Then as if his ears had been burning, a letter came from Cody, and Clever Riley said he was an hour late on his round because he went inside with Katie and they read it together. Katie put on scones and tea with a nip in it and had Clever Riley thinking he was the whole post office system itself and that the bringing of the letter was the most glorious deed in the annals of messenger-carrying.

Cody said he was keeping well. He'd been getting along under his own steam, meeting good hearts and warm hands everywhere; eating by a campfire and using the earth for a bed and the stars for a roof; tramping the roads and riding in trucks. He said he jumped the rattler from Cockburn to Peterborough and it was the coldest ride in Australia bar none; made worse by the fact, said he with a trace of the old humor, that he was lying in an open truck on a bed of lead ore concentrate, gritty as sugar and icy as the moon.

He gave a post office address, and dozens of letters went to him apart from Katie's. The boys told him they missed him and when was he coming back? It was time he got his fighting colors on again and showed them all that you couldn't keep a good man down. They said a lot more than Katie did. She told him she thought he'd been et by blackfellers the time he took to write, but there was always a home for him to come back to when he wanted. She told him just in a hinting way that she was looking around for a boy to lick into shape for a crack at the title, as with the right material it wouldn't be so hard to take it, she thought, but so far she hadn't had any luck. She told him not to leave off his woollen singlets, God-blessed him and finished off.

At the end of six months Cody Codrington came home. He

was lean and grave, still with a lot on his mind and in his heart. There was an older wiser look about him. Gradually he pulled out of his reticence, and it was good to see. He even sang a bit. And he could crack a joke with you when you talked together. Everybody in the know said it was the doing of Katie McGarrigle. But Katie would have none of that. She said it was himself. He saw himself for the wreck he was and was ashamed. He had spirit, she said, and it was his own spirit that was rehabilitating him.

But Cody said his fighting days were finished forever.

He went down to work on the wharves. He wanted to continue the open air life, and he wanted now the friendliness of men. He went to work in a tram and came home in a tram. He looked older than his years, but he was fit. In the home he still felt a resentment against Katie for not liking Judy, his wife. It wasn't a resentment really; it was just a yearning, a wish that it could have been different. If it had, he felt, Katie would now be able to share his memories and thoughts of her, and he wanted that.

One day, in a mood, he brought down the picture of his wife and Barney together and placed it defiantly on the mantelshelf alongside the one of himself as a boy, which Katie had treasured these many years. Katie made no comment. At the end of the week it was still there.

He had been back three months when he came in one evening and brought Barney with him, introduced him to his grandma and told him this was to be his new home.

'It's not that Judy's people don't want him,' Cody said. 'Nobody could have been kinder to him. But I want him with me, and he wants me around, too. It's the best this way.'

He was fond of the boy and he began to observe how Katie treated him. He noticed the treatment was standoffish, matter of fact. Katie cooked for the boy and washed him and tucked him into bed, but she did it all as a hired menial might. Cody wondered whether he was doing the right thing living under the same roof. He was hurt more than worried. Katie never said anything nice about the boy; nor anything nasty, either. She's getting old, he thought, and how do I know what goes on in the mind of an old Irish woman?

He wanted to bridge the gulf and he didn't know how.

So they just went on living, and Jim Kelly, that old pug that nobody remembers now but who was a champion in his time, died in the Old Men's Home, and Cody was the only one at his funeral, and he saw that Jim's old trunks were buried with him the way he wanted; and Jack Haines was fighting for his life in Melbourne, and Cody's boy, Barney, was going to school and doing fine.

One drizzling day Katie McGarrigle heard Barney crying loudly; in fear and alarm she ran out to see him coming through the back gate, his mouth wide open and tears streaming down his pale face.

'Saints alive, what's the matter with you?'

She watched him coming towards her, his muddy, knobbly knees bending with each stride, his hands clenched, arms stiff at his sides.

'Grandma! Oh, grandma!' he sobbed, and clutched her, burying his face in her dress. She looked down at him, her lips quivering, at his black head and little shoulders, sturdy but little, and the whole five years of him thrown at this moment under her protection cut her heart in two.

She bent down and hugged him tightly, and said: 'There, there, be a man now.' She took his hand and led him inside.

'Who hit you?' she said

There was a bruised lump on his cheekbone. 'A big boy,' he said. 'Even bigger'n you.'

'And you ran away, I s'pose?'

'No, I tried to hit him, but he wouldn't stand still and let me.'

'Come in here,' Katie said.

Cody came home early that afternoon, for there was no work in the rain; he came through the back gate, a weary man, and at the dining room door heard the thud of gloves in the next room, and the voice of his boy choked with fierce and tearful words of ferocity. He heard the voice of Katie McGarrigle and her saying: 'Oh, you've got your father's right hand; his aggressiveness, too.' And then: 'That'll do, that'll do, Barney. I'm not as fast as I used to be. You'll be all right, boy. There's not many'll lick you when I'm done with showing you how. Shut up now and bring your bloody nose here.'

It was then, in that hour, in that moment, that the last vestiges of the shadow went out of Cody Codrington's life; it was then that the sadness of his past rolled away like a cloud and let a light come upon him: a vitality that seeped warmth into his flesh and jigged his nerves with exhilaration. It was then that he saw the bridge to his future, and then that the courage, the desire, the inspiration of the past repossessed him once more.

No matter who tells you different it was then, God's truth, that Cody Codrington listened excitedly to the urging of ambition and resolution that led to his comeback. It brought him to that night in September when, with Katie in his corner, he danced out to conquer, and went on conquering until it was time to pull out undefeated and give himself over to bringing up his son and caring for an old blind woman till the end of her days.

But he could know nothing of these truths then. All he could do was stand there and wonder, like a man come upon the secrets of peace and love. He heard the sniffling in the next room and the soothing words, and a soft, reflective smile came over his face. His eyes fell on the picture of himself as a boy, and alongside it on the mantelpiece, the one of his wife and son, and in a little while he couldn't see them.